BEYOND *the* BASES

OUT OF REACH BOOK ONE

NEW YORK TIMES BESTSELLING AUTHOR

KAYLEE RYAN

Cover Design: Sommer Stein, Perfect Pear Creative Covers
Cover Photography: Sara Eirew
Editing: Hot Tree Editing
Formatting: Integrity Formatting

BEYOND
the BASES

OUT OF REACH BOOK ONE

KAYLEE RYAN

CHAPTER 1
Easton

I TILT THE BOTTLE TO my lips as I listen to my best friend and teammate, Andrew 'Drew' Milton, yammer on about some chick he hooked up with while we were on the road. Drew is what you would call a hookup artist. He's bagging girls in every city.

"I'm telling you, East, you don't know what you're missing," he says before finishing off his own beer.

"I do fine on my own," I remind him.

"Fine." He says the word as if he's never heard it before. "Fine is for frog hair." He grins, his Alabama country boy roots showing. "Grade A, all you can eat, is what I'm talking about."

My lips tip up into a smile. I can't help it. "Just because I don't broadcast it, doesn't mean I'm not getting it." While lately I've been in a dry spell, I can't help but wonder what it would be like to have just one woman. Someone to trust to be there regardless of my job. Someone who wants me outside of the balance in my bank account.

"Right." He laughs. "How long has it been? Weeks? Months? Fuck, man, your dick is going to fall off from not using it."

"Do you hear yourself right now?" I ask, amused. "My cock is fine, thank you very much."

"Suit yourself." He scoots back from the table. "You want another?"

"Yeah." I reach for my wallet, but he waves me off, heading toward the bar.

Shorty's is a hole-in-the-wall joint here in Nashville. It's off the beaten path, and the patrons, as well as the owner, couldn't give a fuck that the Blaze players hang out here. Which is precisely why we do it. The fans are great, and with growing up being the son of the Houston Flash's all-star pitcher, I'm not new to the celebrity status. When I signed with the Blaze, I was all for it, lapping up the attention. I was eighteen and went straight to the majors. I was living the dream, or so I thought. Baseball has been my passion since I was a kid. I'm honored to be able to play a sport I love for a living. The rest of it, the attention and the hookups... that shit gets old, fast.

I'm fortunate that my dad taught me everything he knows. He didn't just teach me about the sport, but also the industry. I didn't go crazy like some of the other rookies. I've had my fair share of fun, but some of these guys make hooking up into a sport all of its own. Dad was a family man. I'm sure before he met Mom he was wild and crazy, but those stories are buried under a rock somewhere.

I finish off my beer and let my eyes roam the dark room. There are a few regulars playing pool on a table that looks to be as old as I am. There's duct tape around the legs, holding it together. Besides that, there's a dartboard that hangs a little further to the left than it should, but no one seems to care that it's crooked. They continue to toss darts night after night. There are several small, round tables, and chairs with scratched legs. The bar itself is also wooden, with chips and carvings into the grain of the wood.

There's a single flat-screen TV that hangs over the bar. More than likely, you can find a game of some sort playing at all times. Billy, the owner, is a sports nut. When I started playing for the Blaze, and the guys asked me out for a drink, they assured me that no one would bother us. I didn't believe them, we were the Blaze after all, but they were right. Billy apparently threatened to kick anyone out years ago who bothered any of the Blaze players. Over the years, there have been a few newbies, and he's the first to put them in their place or kick their asses to the curb. It's nice to have a place to unwind and not have to deal with the masses.

My eyes sweep past the door and then back. Two women who I've never seen before just walked in. We're here a lot, enjoying the anonymity and all that. Very rarely is there a face I don't recognize, and none ever as gorgeous as these two.

"What are you...?" Drew's voice trails off when he follows my gaze. "Damn."

They're both gorgeous, but I can't seem to take my eyes off the brunette. I watch as her friend links their arms together and guides them to the bar.

"I call—" Drew starts, but I stop him.

"The brunette is mine," I say, not giving him a chance.

"Hell yeah." He claps his hands, rubbing them together. "That's what I'm talking about."

I don't dignify his reaction with a response. Instead, I watch them. The blonde friend orders them drinks, and I'm surprised they both receive a bottle of beer. *My kind of girl.* They turn to look for a table, and Drew stands and saunters over to them.

"Would you ladies like to join us?" I hear him ask. Drew doesn't know the meaning of inside voice.

The blonde immediately nods while the brunette looks a little less certain. She does, however, follow her friend to the table. I stand to greet them, holding my hand out to the blonde first. "Easton," I say, shaking her hand.

"Chloe, and this is Larissa." She releases my hand and motions toward the brunette.

"Hey," I say, my voice more gravely than I'd like. "Easton." I offer the lovely Larissa my hand. Hers is soft and smooth, a definite contrast to mine, which are hard and calloused from years of playing ball. Remembering my manners, I pull the chair out for her. She eyes me skeptically, but takes the offered seat.

"So, are you ladies new in town?" Drew asks.

"Nah, I've lived here my entire life," Chloe offers.

"What about you?" I ask Larissa.

"Yeah, born and raised," she says with a soft smile.

"I've never seen you here before," I tell her.

She tucks a strand of hair behind her ear, and I can see a slight tremble in her hands. "I don't really get out much."

"Yeah, I had to beg and plead to get her to come with me tonight," Chloe adds.

"Not much on the bar scene?" I ask Larissa. I know the answer, just by her reactions. She's not some barfly who's playing coy; she really doesn't seem to be comfortable being here.

"Other obligations," she answers.

"So y'all come here a lot?" Chloe asks.

"You could say that." Drew smirks. He's evasive, but his smirk tells me that he knows if this girl tries to hound him here, Billy, also known as Shorty, will kick her ass out.

I keep my attention focused on Larissa. "So, what do you do?"

"I'm a waitress right now. I'm working my way through school. Slowly," she adds.

"What's your major?" She's quiet, and not vying for my attention. That's not something I'm used to.

"Accounting. I'm good with numbers." She shrugs before taking a sip of her beer. "What about you?"

I debate on whether or not to tell her the truth, but she doesn't seem starstruck like so many others. I decide to go for it. "I play baseball."

She raises her eyebrows.

I throw my head back and laugh. "True story. I play first base for the Tennessee Blaze."

She looks at me then to Drew and Chloe. "What?" Drew asks.

"What do you do for a living?" she asks him.

He looks at me, and I give him a subtle nod. "Third baseman for the Tennessee Blaze."

Drew gives zero fucks about shouting from the rooftops about what we do. Me, on the other hand, I sometimes like to just be Easton. In my family, that's how things work. No matter what your profession, you're still just one of the Monroes. "I can get you tickets to a game," I tell her.

"Uh-huh." She nods, a small smile playing on her lips.

She doesn't believe me, and that's okay. What's more important is to keep her talking. I need to know more about her. For example, do her brown locks with a hint of gold feel as soft as they look? How will her lips feel pressed against mine? What does she look like underneath all those clothes? That's a start, but I'm intrigued by the brown-haired beauty who is working her way through college and what her other obligations are that keep her from frequenting bars.

"So which restaurant do you work at?"

"The Vineyard," she says, not taking her eyes off her beer bottle where she's currently peeling back the label.

I whistle. "Nice place. I've been there a few times." This gets me a nod, but that's it. What's it going to take to get to this girl? Looking across the table, I see Drew huddled up close with Chloe, and they're deep in conversation. What is it about Larissa that has me off my game tonight? Finishing off my beer, I stand. "Anyone ready for another?"

Drew holds up two fingers, and I know he's ordering for Chloe too. "You?" I ask Larissa.

"I really shouldn't," she says, lifting her bottle and taking the final sip. I watch as she tilts her head back, the long column of her throat exposed. My lips ache to kiss her, to taste her skin.

Bending down, placing my lips next to her ear, I whisper, "I'll be right back." She can't hide the way her chest inflates with her heavy breath or the way goose bumps break out across her skin. I make my way to the bar and order four bottles of beer, all the while trying to hide my smile. She's more affected than she lets on. When I turn to head back to the table, I see the girls are gone. Quickly, I scan the room and find them huddled over the old jukebox in the corner.

"So, your girl's hot," Drew says when I set two bottles of beer in front of him.

"Her name is Larissa," I remind him.

He holds his hands up like he didn't mean to offend me. "Good to see you back in the game, brother," he says before taking a long pull from his bottle.

"I'm not back in the game. It's not a game, and if it was, I could say I never left. I don't make a sport of dating and hooking up."

"Not now."

He's right. When I was a rookie, I ate that shit up, but it got old, and it's hard to hear Mom call and ask about "all the women." I hate to hear the disappointment in her voice. I've heard whispered stories about my dad and my uncles and their antics all my life, but I've never really seen that from them. They've always been madly in love with their wives. My grandparents are the same way too. I grew up surrounded by couples who are blissfully happy. I've had my fun, not that I'm against more of it, but one day I'd like to find someone to take home to my family.

"Good choice," Drew says when the girls join us. It's an old Aerosmith song, "Dream On," that you can't help but sing along to.

Chloe points across the table. "That's all Larissa. She's the music guru."

"What's your favorite genre?" I ask.

She smiles over at me. "All of it. Well, I'm not much on the super heavy metal stuff. It gives me a headache. Other than that, I'm a fan."

"Really? You go to a lot of concerts?"

"Not really. No time."

When the song changes to Cole Swindell's "Middle of a Memory," I can't fight my smile. Standing, I offer my hand to Larissa. Drew catches on and does the same with Chloe.

"What?" Larissa asks, her green eyes staring up at me.

"Dance with me."

She looks around nervously. "There's no dance floor."

"Doesn't matter." Drew and Chloe head to the darkened corner, leaving us alone. "Dance with me," I repeat. Reluctantly, she places her hand in mine and allows me to guide her to the same corner Drew and Chloe disappeared into. My hands on her hips, I pull her close and sway to the music. I listen to the lyrics and think about how they relate to me, to us in this very moment. There is something about this girl that grips me.

"I feel like everyone's watching us," she says, glancing around.

"Hey," I whisper, and wait until she's looking at me. "There's no one watching you but me. It's just us, right here, right now. Making memories." I wink, and her lips tilt in a smile.

"Are you always this charming? Or just when you're on the prowl?"

"On the prowl?" This girl is a ball buster.

"Yeah, isn't that what you're doing? Trying to sweeten me up so when you ask me to go home with you later, I'll go willingly?"

"Are you suggesting that I would force you to go otherwise?"

"Not at all. I just meant, if you're sweet and charming, you assume my answer will be yes."

"Would it be?" I know the answer is a resounding no.

"No."

"Good thing that's not what I'm doing then, huh?" I give her hip a gentle squeeze.

"Right." She laughs. "I'm the first baseman for the Tennessee Blaze, and we're making memories," she coos, mocking me.

I don't bother to hide my grin. "So, you think this is all talk, just to get you into my bed?"

She shrugs. "If the shoe fits."

"We fit," I say, pulling her tight against me. The subtle hint of warm vanilla assaults my senses. Her hands, which were resting against my chest, snake up around my neck. I could pull out my phone and type my name into the search engine and prove her wrong, but I don't. Instead, I sing along to the song, my voice just low enough for her to hear. I like the thought of just being Easton to her. I like it a whole hell of a lot.

When the song is over, I don't let go. She's going to have to be the one to break this connection. It's been too damn long since a woman has felt this right in my arms. Then again, has it ever felt this right? Chloe appears beside us and pulls Larissa with her to the restroom. I watch them disappear down the hall before going back to our table. Back at the table, Drew sets three fresh beers down, keeping the fourth for himself.

"We're getting ready to head out," he says.

"You and Chloe?" I clarify. I'm not leaving here until Larissa does.

"Yep," he says, popping the *p* and grinning like a fool. "I'm sure they're discussing it now."

"Ready?" Chloe asks, sneaking up on us.

"Got you another." Drew points at the three bottles on the table. I have yet to touch mine.

"We're going to drop Larissa off at her place," she tells him, ignoring the beer.

"I can take you," I offer. "I've only had two." I point to the bottles on the table.

"That's sweet of you, but not necessary."

I stand and grab her hand. "I'd like to." I'm not ready to end my time with her.

She gives me a smile, one that says, "I appreciate the offer, but it's not happening." Her words confirm the look. "Really, I'm good. We live in the same complex, so it's a wasted trip."

"Can I see you again?" I ask her.

"I don't think that's a good idea."

"Are you seeing someone?" *Please say no.*

"No."

"We could have dinner," I suggest.

"Other obligations." She shrugs.

Defeated, I watch as the girls turn and walk away. "Catch you later," Drew says, finishing off his beer and setting the empty bottle on the table. He doesn't comment on me being shut down.

I watch them go, debating on whether I should follow them, follow her and try again. It's not often in this town, or others, that people don't recognize me, either from my family or from my career. She's like a fucking needle in a haystack. One I'll never find again.

CHAPTER 2
Larissa

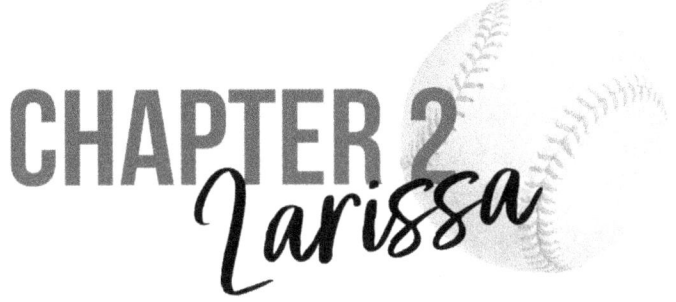

"I STILL CAN'T BELIEVE YOU turned him down," Chloe says.
It's been a week since I let her talk me into a night out, and
this is what I've heard every day since. "You know I have
no room in my life for more complications."

"Complications," she scoffs. "I didn't say to marry the guy, just
get back on the horse so to speak, and trust me, if he's anything like
his friend, you really, really wanna ride the horse." She winks.

"I'm good, thanks," I say, rolling my eyes.

"I'm worried about you."

"Chloe, I'm good. My days are full right now, and I'm okay
with that. I have a plan. I need to finish school. I want better than
this." I motion to the room with my hand. Chloe and I both work
at The Vineyard. It's a swanky upscale restaurant here in
Nashville. It's good money, but the nights and weekends are
grueling. Add school and family obligations on top of that and,
well, there just isn't much time for anything else.

"I know you do. We both do. You're working yourself to the bone trying to do it all on your own."

"And what choice do I have in that?" I snip. I don't mean to be short with her, but she knows how crazy things are for me right now.

"Look, Larissa, I'm sorry. You're the strongest, most dedicated person I know. I just want to see you happy."

"And you think hooking up with some random guy in a bar who claims to be a major league baseball player will make me happy?"

"What do you mean, 'claims to be'? They are," she informs me.

"You've got to be kidding me. Please don't tell me you fell for that line?"

"Babe, I hate to break it to you, but you're wrong on this one."

"Hey, Larissa, I just seated a party of four in your section," Tara, the hostess, informs me.

It's been a slow night so far, so I'm thankful for something to do to get away from Chloe's inquisition. "Thanks, Tara. As for you"—I point at my best friend—"don't fall for every line they tell you."

She laughs. "Go get your drink orders, and by the time you come back, I'll have proof." She holds up her phone.

"Don't you have tables to serve or something?"

"Nope. I'm gonna sit right here and get my proof ready."

Shaking my head, I head toward my table of four. I block out my conversation with Chloe and place a smile on my face. "Welcome to The Vineyard. I'm Larissa. I'll be your server," I say while flipping my order pad to a clean page to take their drink orders. When I look up, my smile falters just a little before I catch it and correct myself.

"Hey, Ris." Easton smiles up at me. "Fancy meeting you here." His grin is infectious.

"Good to see you again," I say, then glance at the other three guys. They're all built and hot as hell. "Drew." I smile at him.

"Tonight we have spare ribs." I go on to tell them the special of the day ignoring my rapidly beating heart. "Can I start you off with drinks?" I start from right to left, ending with Easton. "Take your time looking over the menu. I'll be right back with your drinks." Slowly, I turn and walk away. Once I'm out of their sight, I rush to the back room where Chloe and I were taking our break. Leaning my back against the wall, I close my eyes and will my heart to slow. What are the chances of him showing up here?

"Hey, take a...." She trails off when she sees my face. "What's up?"

"Oh, you know, nothing except Easton, Drew, and two other guys who are disturbingly just as gorgeous are my table of four."

"Damn. You have all the luck. I'll have to swing past and say hello to Drew. Maybe he'll want to get together tonight. Anyway, look at this." She thrusts her phone in my face.

It takes a minute for my eyes to focus, but when they do, my mouth drops open. There, on the tiny screen, is a picture of Drew and Easton in matching Tennessee Blaze uniforms. My eyes scan the article quickly. It's from last year when they won the World Series. *Holy shit!*

"And I believe this is where I say I told you so." She laughs.

"Okay, so he was honest about that, but come on, Chloe. Think about this for a minute. Guys like them can have anyone they want. Why some random stranger at a bar? Oh, that's right, they want to get their dick wet. Case in point, you took Drew home with you."

"You're damn right I did, and it was ah-maz-ing. You need to have a little fun in your life, Larissa. Knock off the cobwebs." She grins, placing her phone back in her pocket.

"Hey, Chloe, table of two," Tara announces on her way to the kitchen.

"I might just have to take the long way to my section," she says, sauntering away.

I watch her go, still in disbelief that Easton plays for the Blaze. Shaking myself out of my thoughts, I gather their drinks, steel my features, and head back to their table. I can feel his eyes on me as I pass out drinks. "Are you ready to order?" I again start on the left, ignoring his penetrating gaze. I focus on taking their orders, then turn to Easton. "For you?" I ask politely.

"What do you recommend?"

"The spare ribs are an excellent choice. We also have a great sirloin. You can cut it with a fork." I tell him my usual spiel.

"I'll take the sirloin," he says.

"Ten ounce or twelve?"

"Twelve."

"How would you like that cooked?"

"Well done. Baked potato, butter and sour cream, broccoli, and salad with ranch."

I work on writing down his order, knowing he's still watching me. When I look up, he's smiling with the menus in hand.

"Here you go." He hands them to me.

"I'll be right out with your salads." I rush away to put their order in and get a break from his stare. At the computer, I enter their order then place the menus back on the bin, but something catches my eye. Pulling open the top menu, I find a piece of paper with a number on it and a little baseball flying through flames. The Blaze. I can't help but laugh at his hint. Of course, he couldn't write his name. His number falling into the wrong hands would be a nightmare for him I'm sure. It's not the official Blaze logo, but I get the point.

"Table of one," Tara says, smiling.

Quickly, I shove the paper in my pocket and head to my table of one. I smile when I see Mr. Brown. He's a regular here, a widower who lost his wife of forty-eight years. He comes here once a week to have dinner. He told me how this was her favorite place in town to eat, and he comes here for her. One day, when life slows down and I feel like I get a minute to breathe, I want to find a love like that.

I take Mr. Brown's order and rush to get his drink. I scan Easton's table and see how they're doing on drinks without stopping. Minimal communication is key here. I gather a refill for each of them, as well as Mr. Brown's sweet tea and water with lemon, and place them on my tray.

"How about some refills?" I ask. I don't make eye contact with any of them while I set their drinks down.

"Thanks, Ris." Easton smiles.

All I can do is nod and try to act as if his smile doesn't make my belly quiver. As I head to my next table, I think about how much I love that he shortens my name, but I'll never tell him that. I've always just been Larissa to my family and friends. "Here you go, Mr. Brown. Your salad should be out soon."

"Thanks, dear." He smiles kindly.

As I walk back through the dining area, I feel a hand grab mine, stopping me in my tracks. Looking down, I see Easton holding onto my hand. "What time do you get off tonight?" His brown eyes are pleading for me to tell him.

His buddies make some lewd jokes at his question, and honestly, it's hard for me not to smile as well. He kind of walked into that one. He whips his head around and gives them what I imagine is a "shut the hell up" look before turning back to face me. "Maybe we can go for coffee or something after?"

"Can't. Thank you though." I pull my hand from his and walk away, rushing back to the lounge, as we like to call it. It's really just a place for the staff to wait so we're not seen lurking around. We have screens on the walls that show us our customers, making it so we don't have to hover: the perks of an upscale restaurant. Leaning my back against the wall, I take a deep breath and slowly exhale.

"What's wrong?" Chloe asks.

"You need to take over my table," I tell her. He's too sexy, too charming, and I can't afford that kind of distraction.

"Can't. I have a party of eight. You know how confusing that gets, switching in the middle. Why, what happened?"

"Easton happened. He's determined to keep asking me out. He slipped me his number then stopped me as I was walking by, asking me if I wanted to go out for coffee when I get off tonight." Hell yes, I want to go. There's not a female on the planet who wouldn't want to go. I, however, can't get caught up in him. Not now. I have too much going on in my life to fall for some famous athlete just to have my heart broken in the end. I don't have time for heartbreak, or games for that matter. My life is way too complicated for that.

"And you said yes, right?" she asks, hopeful, but I can see it in her eyes that she already knows my answer.

"You know I can't."

"I know you can, but you refuse to. You have to live life, Larissa. My fear is one day you're going to wake up and wonder what might have been."

"Sure, what might have been heartache from letting a famous athlete fool me into thinking I could be enough for him," I scoff.

"Do you know him?" she challenges me.

"You know I don't."

"Then you don't know what his intentions are. You don't know what kind of guy he is. You know what you've heard about athletes like him, but I know you're smart enough to understand that the tabloids print complete shit. Listen, I need to get to my table, but you need to think about this. Give him a chance and feel out the situation before you jump to the conclusion that he's some player on and off the field." I watch as she turns and walks away.

Sucking in a deep breath, I compose myself. I have to serve them until they're gone, so I'm just going to have to deal. He'll be gone once they're finished, and then everything will be right in my world. Although, right now it feels like my world is tilted on its axis and one wrong move could send me tumbling into an abyss.

CHAPTER 3
Easton

"SHE SHOT YOU DOWN, MONROE," Carr says, before biting down on his fist to keep from laughing.

"Yeah, you assholes didn't help matters much," I grumble. I should have known better than to bring them here.

"She the one you met that night?" Fisher asks.

I nod. They know I met a girl and was shot down, no thanks to Drew. He, of course, has been bragging all week that he took her friend Chloe home with him and that I struck out. I've had to listen to his replay all damn week when all I wanted to do was come here to see if she was working. Just wanting a chance to see her again. A chance to change her mind.

"Here you go," Larissa says, appearing beside us. So lost in my thoughts of her, I didn't realize she was here. She serves each of us and steps back from the table. "Can I get you anything else?"

"Yeah," Fisher speaks up. "Can you please put our boy here out of his misery and go out with him? Or at least give him your number?"

A soft smile pulls at her lips. She opens her mouth to answer him, and her eyes find mine. She looks at me like she's trying to put together a puzzle but doesn't quite have all the pieces. "Trust me, Easton." Her voice is soft, almost fragile, as if one wrong word could break her. "I have more going on in my life than you want to take on. You should count this one as a loss and focus on someone else." That last part is whispered so low I can barely hear her.

"What if I don't want anyone else?" I'm fully aware we're in a crowded restaurant and people are watching. I'm aware that nine chances out of ten this will more than likely end up in the tabloids tomorrow. I also know I don't give a fuck about any of that. All I care about is letting her know I'm serious when I say I want to take her out and get to know her. I'm drawn to her. The need to know more about her is just that—a need. The want is there too.

She shakes her head as if she can't believe my question. "Maybe not," she finally says. "But you also don't want me." She stands to her full height and looks over at my three teammates. "I'll be back with some refills," she informs them before turning on her heel and walking away.

"She's a tough nut to crack," Carr says.

"Her friend, not so much," Drew adds.

"Hey, guys," said friend greets us. Chloe smiles over at Drew before making eye contact with each of us.

"Hey, gorgeous," Drew greets her, reaching out and grabbing her hand.

"What kind of trouble are the four of you getting into tonight?" she asks.

"No trouble," I assure her. "Just having dinner."

She laughs. "Right. I've heard that one before. You giving my girl a hard time?" she asks me.

"More like she's giving him one," Fisher speaks up. "Help a guy out, would you? He's been moping around all week since she shut him down, and after tonight's loss, I'm afraid he's going to get a complex."

Chloe turns her attention back to me. "Don't give up on her." She looks over her shoulder, then back to me. "She's got a lot going on, and she's jaded from life itself. If you're serious and want to get to know her, don't give up on her."

Her attention is pulled away when Drew asks, "What time do you get off tonight?"

"I don't know, you tell me," she flirts back.

He throws his head back in laughter. "Text me when you're done. I'll swing by and pick you up."

"I'm out of here at eleven tonight."

"What about Larissa?" I ask.

"She's off at eleven as well," she says with a knowing smile. She's walking away before I can thank her for the intel.

"So what are you going to do about it?" Drew asks.

"I'm gonna be here waiting on her." Honestly, I'm not sure what else I can do, other than being persistent, and I'm not sure that will work with her. She doesn't seem to be impressed that I'm a professional athlete or that my last name is Monroe, hell I'm not even sure she knows who I am. What she doesn't realize is that ramps up her hotness factor and makes me want her even more.

Glancing down at my watch, I see it's nine thirty. I have an hour and a half until I make my next move. The guys and I eat dinner, talking about the season so far, laughing, and cutting up, enjoying our two-day break. Larissa periodically stops and checks on us, getting us refills without asking.

"Who left room for dessert?" she asks, gathering our empty plates.

"I don't see you on the menu," Carr tells her. Without thinking, my arm flies out and I punch him in the arm. "What the fuck?" he asks, rubbing his arm. I shoot him a murderous look, and he clamps his mouth shut.

"I'll take the strawberry cheesecake," Drew tells her.

"Make that two," Fisher chimes in.

"For you?" she asks Carr.

"Peanut butter silk pie." He winks at her, and I'm tempted to hit his ass again. Apparently, it wasn't hard enough the first time.

"Easton?" The sound of my name on her lips is something I want to hear more of.

"Oreo cheesecake, please," I say, handing her the dessert menu.

"Great. I'll be back in a few." She turns and leaves.

I turn my attention to Carr. "What the fuck was that?"

"What? I was just messing with both of you."

"Not with her," I tell him. He holds his hands up, telling me he understands and he's going to back off. I'm into this girl. I want to explore whatever this is, and I don't need his dumb ass making it harder for me than it already is.

A few minutes later, she's back and setting our desserts in front of us. "Enjoy." She's gone as quickly as she arrived, not even giving me time to say thanks.

The guys and I shoot the shit for a little while longer until Larissa appears with our checks. "I got it," I tell her, handing over my credit card. She takes it and disappears around the corner.

"Thanks for dinner, man." Drew nods in my direction.

"I needed to make sure she was tipped well," I tell him.

"What, you think we're cheap?" Fisher asks, looking amused.

"I know you are, unless you're certain to get something out of it," I fire back.

"She might pick me," he says, already laughing at his own joke.

"Dude, did you see him hit me? That shit hurts." Carr rubs his arm again to get his point across.

"Come on, Monroe. We're fucking with you. You're in knots over this girl, which is new. We have to give you shit," Fisher chimes in.

"Just don't give it to her," I warn.

"Here you go. Thanks for coming in. Have a good night." She drops off my receipt and credit card then walks away.

I sign the bottom of the receipt, leaving her a hefty tip. "You waiting here?" I ask Drew as we walk outside.

"Yeah, might as well. You?"

"Yeah, I don't want to chance missing her." Plus, if I'm with Drew, I'm hoping I look less stalkerish.

"The black Impala is Chloe's." He points to the back part of the lot that's darker than I'd like knowing the girls walk out alone at night.

"I guess we should park over there." I don't wait for his reply. Instead, I climb into my truck and drive around the lot. I park beside the Impala, and Drew parks beside me. I know I should have let him be right next to her, but he has an advantage over me. One, he knows what she drives, and two, she's more than willing to go out with him. I'm not that lucky.

Climbing out of the truck, I round the back and drop the tailgate. Drew joins me as we wait for the girls to get off work, while Fisher and Carr head to Shorty's. I'm sure I'll get shit for it later. Drew, on the other hand, will not. He's waiting for his hook-up. Me, I'm just waiting for a girl who apparently wants nothing to do with me. We're in the middle of debating our rookie outfielders this season when the back door of the restaurant opens and slams shut, the sound echoing through the night sky.

"Go time," Drew says, rubbing his hands together.

I don't take my eyes off her as she walks toward us. Her step falters when she notices me. I hop off the tailgate and meet her halfway. "Hey," I say, stopping in front of her. Her hair is falling out of her ponytail and into her eyes. Reaching out, I tuck it behind her ear. "Long night?" I ask like an idiot. Nothing I say works with this girl.

"You could say that," she admits. "What are you doing, Easton?"

"I wanted to see you."

"You've seen me. Now if you'll excuse me, I really need to go." She moves to step around me, and I follow her. She stops next to an older model Ford Escape.

"Tell me what I need to do." I step up next to her. "What's it going to take for you to give me a shot?"

"There is no chance." She sighs and turns to face me. "Look, I'm sure you're a great guy, but my life is complicated. I can't let myself get wrapped up in you. I don't have time for the heartache."

Heartache? This feeling deep in my gut tells me that any amount of time spent with her would be my undoing. This would be more than just a one-night stand. Reaching out, I catch her hand and lace my fingers through hers. "Who says it's going to end in heartache?"

"Let's be real here, Easton. You're a major league baseball player. I'm just a girl trying to make ends meet while working toward her degree. Our lives are too different," she says. I can tell she means it; she truly feels like our lives are too different, but her reaction to my touch, the fact that she doesn't pull away... the way her eyes are pleading yet hopeful at the same time.... That tells me more than her words ever could.

"Not so much. My job doesn't define who I am, Larissa."

"Maybe not, but it's a risk I can't afford to take."

My first thought is that she's been hurt in the past. Why else would she label me... us a risk? She thinks her words will push me away when in fact they just pull me in closer. I want to know her past. What has happened in her life for her to be so guarded? What can I do to take that fear away? "Just one dinner." My voice is pleading, and I realize how pathetic it makes me look, but I'm desperate for more time with her. She's bewitched me.

"I'm sorry." She smiles sadly. "I just... can't. Thank you for the offer." My heart sinks and I know I've lost her. There's finality in every syllable. "It's flattering." It's with those parting words that she climbs in her SUV and pulls out of the lot.

I stand and watch her go. When her taillights disappear into the dark of night, I head back to my truck. Drew and Chloe are already gone. At least they weren't here to witness my epic fail. Then again, even if they were here, it wouldn't stop me from pursuing her. She needs to know I'm not a man who gives up that easily. I have no problem fighting for what I want. She's what I want. I just have to find a way to show her my words aren't empty. I mean everything I say. *Speak from your heart,* my mother always used to say. Climbing in my truck, I head toward home. It's time to figure out my next move.

CHAPTER 4
Larissa

I TOSSED AND TURNED ALL night. I kept seeing Easton and those big brown eyes as he pleaded with me to give him a shot. Turning him down was hard, but it's what I needed to do. He's too charismatic, too gorgeous. I could get caught up in him too easily. I'm not ready for that. I have a plan and need to stay focused.

The house is quiet, normal for six in the morning. My alarm's set for six thirty, so I reach over and turn it off. No use in trying to go back to sleep, not after the restless night I had. I can't stop thinking about him. The way his eyes roam over me, both sexual and in a way no one has ever looked at me. The way my skin heats and prickles with awareness anytime he's near. Easton Monroe is a hard man to resist. Throwing off the covers, I head to the shower. I might as well get moving. Maybe I can get some studying in before I have to leave for class.

On the way to school, I call Mom and check in on things. "Good morning," I greet her.

"You sound tired," she answers. I never could get anything past her.

"I didn't sleep the greatest last night."

"What's going on?" Concern laces her voice.

"Nothing, just couldn't sleep. How are things?"

"Good. Getting ready to fix us some breakfast. Did you eat?" She's always worrying about me.

"I grabbed a granola bar on my way out the door. I only have morning class today and then I'll swing by your place. I have to be at work at four."

"I still think you should move in here, let us help you while you focus on your degree." This isn't a new conversation. It's one we've had many times over the last few years.

"Mom, I appreciate that more than you know. You already do so much for me and I like having my own space. It's good to know that if I need to, I can always come home."

"If you change your mind...."

"I know, thank you. I'm at school. I need to get to class. I'll see you later."

"Have a good day, sweetheart."

I make it to class just as the professor starts his lecture. Business ethics is not a hard class, but it's not one that is particularly engaging either. It's a means to an end, which is earning my bachelor's degree in accounting. I'm taking notes and trying like hell not to fall asleep when my phone vibrates in my purse at my feet. Slipping it out of my purse, I see a text message from Chloe. I don't bother reading it, needing to focus extra hard on the class; instead, I toss my phone back in my purse. I only have twenty minutes of this class left, and if I reply, I'm sure to miss that last part of this lecture. Just my luck that's what we'll be tested over.

I'm packing up my bag when my phone vibrates with a call. I don't even bother looking; I know it's Chloe. "Hey, you're persistent this morning."

"So, I met up with Drew last night."

"I was there, remember?" I can already tell where this call is going. She wants me to take Easton up on his offer.

"I asked him what Easton's deal was."

"You called me as soon as my class was over, the exact minute to tell me you decided to be nosey and inquire about your booty call's friend?" I'm being a sassy bitch, but she knows why I can't do this.

She laughs. "You're damn right I did. Anyway, Drew says he's into you."

"How can he be 'into me'? He doesn't even know me."

"You know what I mean. He really wants to get to know you. Drew says he's a good guy."

"Right, said the serial killer's best friend."

"Aren't we a little testy today?" she teases.

I release a heavy breath. "I'm sorry. I'm exhausted. I got maybe a couple hours of sleep last night at best."

"Is everything okay?"

"Yeah, you know the house was quiet and I was just... thinking."

"Uh huh. Thinking about a tall, dark-haired, baseball-playing drink of water, were you?"

"I admit he's easy on the eyes, but the mature, responsible version of me knows that this entire situation has bad idea written all over it. You know I have so much going on in my life. I can't get caught up in him. I don't have time for heartbreak." I'm well aware my words are on a constant repeating loop with all the reasons why I can't allow myself to be involved with not just Easton, but anyone. My hope is that if I say it enough, people will get the message loud and clear and believe it. Maybe if I say it aloud enough, I'll even start to believe it. I would love to throw caution to the wind and see where things go. That's just not an option for me at this point in my life.

"It's not your heart I'm trying to revive. It's the girly bits. If you don't dust the cobwebs off soon, I'm afraid you'll never find it."

"Ha ha, smartass. Was there another reason for your call?"

"Wanna get lunch?" she asks, not missing a beat.

"I told Mom I would stop by. Speaking of, she's beeping me now. Hold on a sec." I pull the phone away and click the Accept Call button on the screen. "Hey, Mom, I'm headed that way."

"That's why I'm calling. We decided to go to Jackie's." Jackie's my aunt, Mom's older sister. "We're not there. Take a nap, enjoy a couple of hours of free time before work."

"Are you sure?"

"Positive. I'll see you in the morning."

"Okay, I'll call before my shift."

"Bye now," she says, ending the call.

"You there?" I ask Chloe.

"Yeah, everything good?"

"They decided to go to Aunt Jackie's so I have the afternoon free. I'm at work at four."

"I'm on tonight too," Chloe tells me.

"I thought you were off?"

"I traded with Sasha. Her son's sick. So, lunch?"

"Sure, where do you want to meet?"

"How about Shorty's? I'm telling you, their food is delicious. Don't let the rundown bar motif scare you away."

I mull this over. Surely the chances of running into Easton and his crew in the middle of the day at Shorty's is unlikely. "Sure. I can be there in twenty minutes."

"Great. I'm closer so I'll grab us a booth."

"See you soon."

"Later," she replies, and the line goes dead. My best friend is a tornado, always has been.

Reaching my car, I toss my bag in the back seat and head toward Shorty's. I'm starving, so the food better be as good as she claims.

The lot is practically empty when I pull in, the inside the same. There are two older gentlemen sitting at the bar. Other than that, it's just Chloe who's in a booth in the back corner.

"Hey, I ordered us some potato skins, and sweet tea to start with. I'm starving."

"Me too. All I've had today is a granola bar." My stomach growls, proving my point, just as the waiter stops by with our potato skins.

"You ready to order?" he asks.

"I'll have the bacon cheeseburger with steak fries," Chloe tells him.

"Make that two." I offer him a smile.

"How was class?" she asks, her eyes flicking over my shoulder to the door. My stomach drops. Surely it's not him. Slowly, I turn to gaze over my shoulder and see a third older gentleman taking a seat at the bar. "Good," I answer, turning back to face Chloe. "Hard to stay awake. It's not exactly engaging material."

"I hate classes like that. Luckily for me, elementary education is not as boring."

"All of it's boring at some point."

"Says the accounting major," she says with a laugh and picks up a potato skin.

I nod, chewing on the delicious morsel "Boring it is," I say after swallowing, "but it's a good field with lots of job opportunities and security. All things I need in my life."

"Is that all you need?" a deep voice asks from beside me.

Slowly, I turn my head and see Drew and Easton standing next to our booth. I open my mouth to reply but words escape me. Looking across the booth at Chloe, she's grinning from ear to ear. I should have known her suggestion to come here of all places was a setup. I want to be mad at her, but the way my pulse quickens at just the sight of him tells me it's no use. I can't help but wish things were different, that I didn't have the worries and fears that plague me. That I had the time and the energy to devote to a man like Easton Monroe.

"Mind if we join you?" Easton asks.

Immediately, Chloe scoots over on her side of the booth, making room for Drew. I do the same, not wanting to be rude. Easton seems like a really nice guy, but life is complicated and messy and just not that easy. At least not for me. It hasn't been that way for a long time.

"What are you all getting into today?" Chloe asks like she doesn't already know. I'd kick her shin if I thought I could get away with it, but knowing my luck, I'll end up hitting Drew instead. So instead, I stare at her, eyes wide, asking her what the hell she was thinking. The look doesn't even faze her as she gives her attention to Drew and Easton, effectively ignoring me.

"Early practice. We're done for the day," Drew says, playing her game.

Grabbing my sweet tea, I take a long drink, keeping my eyes focused on the table in front of me.

Just as I'm setting my glass back on the table, Easton leans into me. His thigh presses against mine, his lips close to my ear. "You okay?" he asks, just low enough for me to hear.

"Fine." I nod, trying to scoot away from him. Unfortunately, the booth does not allow me further escape. Where his body is aligned with mine, it feels as though my skin is on fire.

"What are your plans for the rest of the day?" he asks.

I clear my throat. I can do this. I can be friendly, have lunch, and then be on my way. "I have to study, then be at work by four."

"Accounting, right?" he asks.

I'm surprised he remembers anything we talked about that night. "Yeah, I have two more semesters and then I'm done. I plan to sit for the CPA exam."

"You like numbers, huh?"

I shrug. "I'm good at it, math, algebra, all of it comes pretty easily to me."

"Do you love it? You should be doing something you love."

"It's a good field, with lots of job opportunities and security. I need that more." I look down at my hands that are clasped on the table. My life seems boring compared to his. I'm not embarrassed of who I am, but surely he realizes he's way out of my league after this conversation.

"So you said," he says, referring to the conversation he walked in on. He opens his mouth to say more, but the waiter, Shorty, who I know is the owner, brings the guys two glasses of water each and asks if they want their usual. I take advantage of Shorty holding Easton's attention, and take him in. He's wearing a backwards baseball hat, his dark hair slightly curling just above his ears. His dark eyes are expressive and kind. He's wearing a black form-fitting Tennessee Blaze T-shirt that looks as though it was tailor made to fit him. I can only imagine the amount of time and effort it's taken him to get his body to look like a Greek god's. Then again, he is a professional athlete. When he's here like this, it's hard to remember that. He's just Easton.

Shorty leaves, and Easton turns back to face me and catches me staring. "You come here a lot?" I ask, trying to avoid the fact that I'm busted. It's an obvious answer, but it pulls the conversation away from me.

"We do. Shorty takes care of us. Keeps the fans at bay. The regulars just let us be us. It's a nice change of pace."

I nod like I understand, but truly I have no idea. I can imagine that always being in the spotlight would get old, fast. Just another reason turning him down is a good idea. The remainder of lunch flies by. Chloe keeps the conversation flowing about our classes and work. We see a lot of crazy things working at a fancy restaurant. The audacity of what some people expect blows my mind.

"So if not accounting, then what?" he asks.

"When I was younger, I would have said a photographer. I got a camera for Christmas one year and I took pictures of everything, of nothing," I admit with a laugh.

"And now?" he prompts.

I take a minute to think about my life. I'm twenty-two years old carrying what often feels like the weight of the world on my shoulders. "A mom," I answer him honestly. The words are out of my mouth before I can stop them. I guess it's a good thing really. What young, hot-as-hell professional athlete wants to get involved with a woman who says if she had her choice she would be a stay-at-home mom?

"You like kids, huh?"

"I do. I was an only child growing up. My mom stayed home and was always there. Dad too. He worked long hours, but there was never a major moment in my life that the two of them weren't there." That was the life I envisioned for myself. I wanted what they had, but life always ends up throwing you a curve ball when you least expect it. We lost Dad and our world shattered. To me that was the turning point, and the moment I realized that nothing is guaranteed in life.

He nods like he gets it. "Family is important."

Not long after, Shorty stops to ask if we need anything else, which prompts Drew and Easton to hand over their credit cards, covering our bills.

"So, can I call you?" Easton asks once Shorty walks away, cards in hand.

"Let me give you some money," I reach for my bag, but he places his hand over mine, stopping me.

"Please don't," he says softly. "Let me do this for you."

I nod. "Thank you for lunch."

The corner of his lips tilts up in a smile. "You can thank me by giving me your number," he suggests. I reach for my purse and pull out some cash and hold it out to him. "Okay, I get it. Put your money away. You keep me on my toes, Larissa."

"So it's the challenge, is it? The chase?" I don't know why I asked that. I know the answer. I'm sure women fall at his feet, and his advances are more than welcomed. Maybe if I were in a different place in my life, they would for me too.

Across from us, Drew slides out of the booth offering Chloe his hand, helping her stand. I turn to Easton, waiting for him to move as well, and find him watching me, not making a move to exit the booth. "It's not the chase, Ris." He reaches out and tucks my hair behind my ear. "From the moment I laid eyes on you, I've felt off-center. Like I need to get to know you for my world to be righted once again. I can't explain it, even if I tried. All I know is that it's not the chase, gorgeous, it's you." With that, he slides out of the booth and offers me his hand. I take it, needing his strength to lift me from the seat. I'm reeling from his confession. His words wanting to take root. Already, just after one lunch and his little speech, I'm ready to forget all the reasons why I've been turning him down.

"Ready?" Chloe asks.

"Yeah." I turn to Easton who is still holding my hand. "Thank you for lunch." He nods and releases his hold on me. I walk to the car on shaky legs, which seems to be something that happens a lot when Easton Monroe is around.

CHAPTER 5
Easton

P RACTICE TODAY WAS BRUTAL. THE hot Tennessee sun was scorching. Thankfully, we started at six this morning to try and beat some of the heat. Now, here I am at noon sitting on the couch, soaking up the air conditioning, thinking about Larissa. Drew and the guys wanted me to go for lunch, but I wasn't feeling it. I'm not in the mood for them to give me shit about the girl who and I'm quoting Fisher on this one, "has got me by the balls." I won't deny it. Well, maybe not the balls part, but she's in my head.

It's been a few days since I've seen her, and I can't get our last conversation out of my mind. She asked me if it was the chase, and I'm certain it's not. However, all I've thought about since she asked me is her and what it is about her that draws me in. Stating the obvious… she's gorgeous. And it's not the chase, but it's *because* of it. I'm used to women falling at my feet. My dad played in the majors my entire life, so I've been in and out of the spotlight. As soon as they found out who I was, who my family was, they—meaning most women—offered themselves to me on a silver platter. I took full advantage in my younger years, and hell, even my first year in the majors, but just as fast as the fame and the women came, the novelty wore off. I grew up in a large family full of men who worshiped their wives, and it's hard to not want that for myself. The past couple of years, I've steered clear of groupies. Sure, there's the occasional hook-up but nothing like the majority of my teammates.

It wasn't until I first laid eyes on Larissa, that I started really thinking about what it would be like to have that one person, all of my own. Someone to come home to after a long stint on the road. Someone to share my nights with, and the offseason. The more I think about it, the more the idea forms a foundation. The only problem is that in those daydreams, all I see is her.

Larissa.

And she wants nothing to do with me. At least that's what she wants me to believe. I can see it in her eyes, the internal battle she's waging to resist me. I wish I knew what it was that was holding her back. If I knew, I could assure her that whatever it is, it's not too big a mountain to climb. Not in the grand scheme of what we could be.

I don't know what it's going to take to get her to take a chance on me.

Flipping through the channels, I stop on an ad for a local florist. The ploy is "let her know you're thinking about her." Normally, I would keep surfing channels, but this time, the commercial works and has me reaching for my phone. I spend the next thirty minutes on the phone discussing the best flowers to send her; the lady on the phone was extremely helpful. She even promised to keep this out of the press. Not that I care about that. I couldn't care less who knows that I'm in knots over this girl. However, my gut tells me that if my interest was to get out, it would push her further away.

They promised delivery to her work today, so I wait to hear from her. The afternoon turns into evening and still nothing. The urge to grab my keys and drive to her work, to be there waiting when she gets off, is strong, but I fight it. I don't want to stalk her. I just want the chance to get to know her. So instead, I settle for watching Sports Center with my phone clutched in my hand, waiting, hoping, wishing she would call. I received an e-mail confirming delivery was made hours ago.

What is it going to take to get her to give me a chance? That's my last thought before drifting off to sleep. Hours later, I'm jolted awake by the alarm on my phone reminding me it's time for my morning run before practice. Silencing the alarm, I turn my head, stretching out the kinks from sleeping on the couch all night. Practice is going to suck. Reaching for my phone, I check my messages and notifications. Nothing from Larissa.

Time for me to step up my game.

CHAPTER 6
Larissa

I T'S SATURDAY AND MY DAY off from the restaurant. I wanted to
sleep in today, but instead, I'm here standing in line, waiting for
further instructions from our group leader, and trying not to
search for him. I tried to think of any excuse to get out of coming
today, but ultimately, this is where I ended up. I changed my outfit
ten times and redid my makeup twice. It has nothing to do with the
fact he might be here—at least that's what I tell myself. Last night I
tried to find a list online of who's participating, but there were no
names listed, just the times of each group's tour.

So here I stand on the Tennessee Blaze field, waiting for our
tour of the stadium to commence. It's one in the afternoon, and
the warm May sun is beating down on us. That's my justification
for sweaty palms, but really, it's him. This is his turf, and he's
been relentless in his pursuit of me. At work two days ago, I
received a bouquet of white roses with a note with the words *To
new beginnings*, and it was signed *East*. He's been back to the
restaurant almost every day the Blaze have been in town. If I'm

not working, he always leaves a note with one of my coworkers to give to me. Chloe thinks I should just give in and go out with him, but I have more than just me to think about. It's easy for someone on their own to forget that.

"Larissa?" his deep voice asks from behind me.

Closing my eyes, I take in a deep breath. Deep down, I knew he would be here. I plaster a smile on my face and turn around. "Hello, Mr. Monroe," I say politely, remembering my manners and why I'm here.

"What are you doing here?"

I'm just about to answer when I'm interrupted. "Mommy, who's that?" my four-year-old daughter, Paisley, asks from beside me. Running my hand over her dark hair, while her big brown eyes pass from me to Easton.

Before I can answer her, Easton drops to his knees and holds out his hand. "I'm Easton, but you can call me East."

I watch as my daughter places her tiny hand in his large one and shakes it. "My name's Paisley Gray. I'm four years old. Are you my mommy's friend? I'm not allowed to talk to strangers," she informs him. Call me a sap, but I have to bite my lip and blink hard to fight back tears. He didn't hesitate to drop to his knees and give her his full attention.

Easton looks up at me and smiles. "It's nice to meet you, Paisley Gray, and yes, your mom and I are friends." His smile causes a flutter in my chest.

Paisley tilts her head to the side and studies him. "Do you play here?" she asks, pointing to the Tennessee Blaze logo on his jersey.

"I do. I play first base."

"Really?" she asks excitedly. "I play too. This is my team." She points to the line of her T-ball team and their parents in front of us. Luckily, we're at the back of the line and they are none the wiser that Easton Monroe, starting first baseman for the Tennessee Blaze, is standing right behind them. At least not yet.

"What position do you play?" he asks her.

"I hit the ball, but I'm not really good at catching it."

He chuckles. "That takes lots of practice."

"Yeah, my mommy's too busy to practice, and Grandma can't catch either," she confesses with a giggle. My heart is in my throat as I watch him interact with my daughter. The fact that I have a daughter doesn't seem to faze him. He talks to her as if he's known her forever and the smile on his face says more than his words. He's not going to let this stop him from pursuing me. I'm not sure how I feel about that. Excited, nervous, scared, elated... I have too many emotions rolling through me all at once.

"If it's okay with your mom, the two of you can stick around today after the tour, and you and I can play catch for a while," he offers.

"Can we, Mommy? Please, can we? Oh please?" she asks, bouncing on the balls of her feet.

"Let's see how the day goes, okay, sweetie?"

"Okay," she says, hanging her head. I hate to disappoint her like that, but neither one of us needs to get close to Easton.

Easton stands to his full height. "It's good to see you," he says, his eyes raking over me. My body reacts to the intensity of his gaze as my cheeks heat. I'm glad I put a little extra time into my appearance today.

"You too." Silence settles between us, neither one of us really knowing what to say.

"She's adorable." He motions to Paisley, who's chatting with one of her teammates. "She looks just like you."

"She has her daddy's eyes," I say, not thinking.

His eyes drop to my hand, I assume looking for a ring. "Is he here?" he asks.

"No, he passed away before she was born." I swallow back the lump in my throat that always rises when I think about him missing out on her life and the void he left us with. My little girl doesn't know what it's like to have a daddy—hell, she doesn't know what it's like to have any male figure at all in her life. This is her first year of T-ball, and her coach is one of the dads, which is really her first true interaction. My dad passed away from a massive heart attack when I was ten.

"Ris." He reaches for my hand, but I step back. His hand drops back to his side, a dejected look on his face.

"The line's moving. I better catch up," I say, realizing that I am in fact losing my group.

"Stay." He places his hand on my arm to stop me. "After, I mean, stay. I'd love to play catch with her," he says, looking at the line where Paisley and her team are starting our tour.

"I really gotta go." I toss him a wave and jog to catch up with my group. Paisley reaches for my hand and swings our arms between us. She's so excited about today, hence the reason I couldn't not go. My arm still tingles from his touch, my heart races in my chest, and my mind swarms in a thousand and one different directions.

"Come on, Mommy," Paisley says, pulling me along.

Shaking myself out of my thoughts, I focus on my little girl and her excitement. We follow along as we walk the bases. The leader of the group, an older gentleman who we learned is retired from the Blaze, explains the importance of each position.

"Who wants to see the locker rooms?" he asks. The kids jump and cheer with excitement. He leads us down a long hall then pushes open the door to the locker rooms. I tune him out, just taking in the room, and that's when I see it. The name Monroe printed over one of the cubbies.

That's his.

That's Easton's.

That's where he prepares before every home game—where he gets dressed after his shower. That thought leads me to water tracing down his toned body, sliding over his muscles that are so obviously visible even beneath his clothes.

"Mommy." Paisley tugs on my hand. "You're not listening," she huffs.

"Sorry, sweetie."

"We're going to see where the hurt players go," she informs me. "Do all players get hurt?"

"No, but with any sport, there's a chance of injury." I try to explain it the best that I can. She shrugs, as if the potential of being injured isn't even on her radar. She can leave the worry up to me; I stress enough for both of us. I mean, it's T-ball, not football, but she's my baby and I worry. That's what I do. It started when my dad passed away. I worried about my mom, about how we were going to make it on our own. I worried about her crying herself to sleep at night. You name it, I worried about it. My anxiety got better as I got older, until the day I opened the front door to a uniformed officer telling me that my husband lost his life in the line of duty. He was a rookie on the force, and his pension was pretty much nonexistent. We had life insurance, but that only lasts so long. We were young and thought we had all the time in the world to plan for retirement and big life insurance policies.

That day brought on an all-new list of worries. How was I going to make it through without the love of my life? How was I going to be a single mother? Could I provide for me and our baby? This time the worry didn't stop; the list has just changed over the years. One that has remained the same is the worry I have for my daughter. The world is a big scary place, and I just want to keep her wrapped in my arms. I want to protect her from anything that could ever hurt her. I know that's unrealistic, but it's always there in the back of my mind.

"Looks like we have a special guest," our tour guide announces, catching my attention. There, standing beside him, is Easton. "Boys and girls, this is Easton Monroe."

The kids cheer, the dads rush to shake his hand, and the mothers, well, all of them except for me, turn on the charm, some of them with their husbands standing right next to them. Me, I stand stock-still in the back of the pack, just watching it all go down.

"That's my mommy's friend. Hi, East," Paisley says at the exact moment our group quiets down. All eyes turn to us. My face heats. My mouth opens, but no words come out.

"Hey, Princess P." Easton waves at her, and she giggles, which in turn causes a smile to cross his handsome face. I keep my eyes straight ahead, avoiding the stares of the other parents.

"Welcome." Easton's deep voice washes over our small group. "For those of you who don't know me, I'm Easton Monroe. I'm the starting first baseman for the Blaze." The group murmurs with hellos and reassurance that they know who he is. "I was hoping to highjack the kids. Me and my teammate, Andrew Milton, thought it would be fun to throw around a few balls with them," he offers.

"Yay!" all the kids cheer, including mine. The parents are quick to agree to this surprise in our agenda. Our leader tells us to follow him to the field. The crowd thins as I stay back, not by choice. Paisley's feet are planted firmly on the ground.

"East," she says once the majority of our group disappears. Easton is still standing there watching us.

He steps toward us and crouches down on his knees, getting more on her level. "What's up, princess?" he asks, melting my heart a little.

Paisley grins up at him. She surprises me when she jumps into his arms, wrapping her arms around his neck. "Thank you," she whispers.

I fight back a sob that threatens to break free. She's never done this before. "You're welcome, sweetheart." He gives her another gentle squeeze then releases his hold on her. "Now, we better get out there before we miss all the fun." He stands and offers her his hand. She takes it without question. I start to warn her about stranger danger, but she knows him as my friend. Easton surprises me when he holds his other hand out for me. He leaves it there, suspended in the air, waiting for me to come to him.

"Come on, Mommy," Paisley coaxes me.

"I'm right behind you," I say, walking toward them, but ignoring his offered hand. He nods in understanding and waits for me to catch up, and the three of us head out to the field. Paisley swings their arms back and forth as she talks Easton's head off about how fun it is to catch and hit the ball. He's patient with her and talks to her as if she knows every detail of the game, when in reality she knows nothing. Her friend Macie begged her to play, and we're just realizing that she loves it. I'm not sure if it's the sport itself or the interaction with the other kids that she loves. She's still too little to tell. Even so, Easton listens to her intently, as if she is well-versed in all things baseball.

I should be mad he's latched onto my daughter, but the smile she's wearing right now takes away any anger I might have had. He's making this day special for her.

CHAPTER 7
Easton

D AMN, THIS LITTLE GIRL IS just like her mother, captivating me from the moment I met her, although in different ways. She's cute as hell as she talks a mile a minute about hitting the ball and catching it. That's the extent of her knowledge, but the way she talks as if she's a little adult, it makes you believe every word she says, as if it's in the rulebooks for the game.

"Can I stay with you?" she asks me once we join her group on a small corner of the field.

"Oh, honey, I don't think—" Larissa starts but stops when I bend my knees and get eye to eye with her.

"I'd really like that, Paisley," I say softly. "But I don't think that would be fair. Everyone needs a turn, and since it's just me and Drew working with your group, you'll have to take turns."

"But you said we could play catch," she says, her little lip quivering.

I look up at Larissa to find her watching us. I raise my eyebrows, and she gives me a slight nod. I mouth "thank you," and turn back to Paisley. No way did I want to tell her no. "How about once the tour is over, you and your mom stick around, and then it will just be you and me? Deal?"

She looks up at her mom, hope shining in her big brown eyes. "Can we, Mommy?"

Larissa nods. "For a few minutes," she adds, but I don't think Paisley hears her or cares. She got the answer she was hoping for and rushes off to join her friends.

"I'm sorry," she tells me.

"Sorry for what?"

"She seems to have taken to you. I know you have more important things to do. We'll just stay a few minutes," she assures me.

Standing, I step in front of her, so close I can feel her hot breath against my chin. "I met this girl," I tell her. "She's beautiful but closed off. I was hoping to drop by her work and catch a glimpse of her since she refuses to go out with me."

"Her life is complicated."

"Life is complicated," I counter. "She's all I think about, and you know what else?" I wait for her reaction. She studies me several long minutes, her breathing labored before she finally answers.

"What?" she asks in a hushed whisper.

"I found out today that she has this amazing little girl, cute as a button, loves baseball." I wink. "I wish she would give me a chance to get to know her, to know both of them."

"She worries," she says, biting her bottom lip.

"About what?" Reaching out, I tuck a loose strand of hair behind her ear.

"Everything."

"Who worries about you?"

Her breath hitches. She opens then closes her mouth, no words coming out.

"Yo, Monroe, you ready?" Drew yells to me.

I hold my hand up in the air, my index finger raised, asking him for one more minute. "Thank you for staying after. We can talk then." I give her hand a gentle squeeze then turn, and walk away, a smile plastered on my face. Not because I'm here in Blaze stadium, my home away from home, but because for the first time I feel like I might be getting somewhere with her.

Drew and I have the group form two lines. There are twelve girls in total on the team, so we each have six. Paisley is in my group; she made sure of it screaming, "I want to be in Easton's group." That little girl is something else. We pitch to them one at a time for about half an hour before they're tuckered out. We sign a few autographs, and they're on their way.

"All right, Miss Paisley, you ready for some one-on-one?" I ask her.

"What's that?"

She acts like she's so much older, talks like it too. I forget she's only four. "That means you and I toss the ball."

"Just us?" she asks, her eyes wide.

"A promise is a promise."

She pulls on the bag that's resting over Larissa's arm. "Mommy, I need my glove," she says excitedly.

Larissa laughs at her daughter; it's a beautiful sound that fills the now quiet stadium. There are still a few players standing around, and the staff, but the rest of the kids and their families are gone. It's just the three of us still messing around out here in the outfield. "Hold your horses," she tells her.

"Mommy, I don't have horses," Paisley says, exasperated, making Larissa and me laugh. Digging in the bag, Larissa reaches her glove and hands it to her daughter. "Ready, East?" she asks me, putting the glove that's a little too big on her tiny hand and reaching for me with the other.

We take a few steps away from Larissa and spread out a little. I'm maybe five feet from her. "Okay, the first thing you want to remember is always have your glove up and ready." I show her what I mean, holding up my glove. "Bend your knees like me," I instruct her. She bends down, legs spread apart, mimicking my stance. "Good job. Now hold your glove up like this," I tell her again. She does as instructed, and I toss her the ball. It hits her glove, and she uses her other hand to keep it inside the glove.

"I did it!" she cheers, jumping up and down, letting the ball fall from her glove.

"You did. You're a natural," I tell her.

"Did your dad teach you how to catch?" she asks innocently.

A smile tilts my lips when I think of my father, Barrett Monroe, and baseball. "He did. Playing baseball was his job." She's a smart little girl, but I'm not sure she would understand if I said he played professionally. "My uncle's played with me as well."

"You have an uncle?" she asks, her eyes wide.

"I do."

"I don't have one of those," she says, looking over at her mom for clarification.

"No, sweetie," Larissa says gently. "Mommy and Daddy were both only children, so you have no aunts or uncles."

"But I want them. Can we get some?" she asks, her innocence grabbing hold of my heart.

"It's not that easy, P. Maybe one day."

"Fine," she grumbles, and I have to bite my tongue to keep from laughing. Little Paisley Gray reminds me so much of her mother.

"You ladies hungry?" I ask them.

"Starving," Paisley says dramatically, dropping her shoulders as if she's been waiting days for me to offer her food.

"How about some pizza? There's a great place just down the street."

"I only like cheese on my pizza. That other stuff is nasty." She wrinkles her little nose.

"Cheese is it." I look over at Larissa. "What do you say? Can I buy you ladies some dinner?"

She opens her mouth to protest, but Paisley beats her to it. "Of course. Mommy says that when people do something nice for you, you say thank you and accept it. Thank you, East," she says, wrapping her arms around my leg in a hug. I smooth back some of her dark curls.

"What do you say, Ris?" I ask, holding my hand out for her.

She looks at me then to her daughter and back to me again. She exhales loudly, as if the words she's about to speak pains her to say them. "Thank you, Easton." Her voice is super sweet with a hint of sarcasm that her daughter doesn't pick up on. To my surprise, she takes my offered hand, and her palm fits against it as if we're two puzzle pieces meant to be together. With a smile on my face and a gorgeous girl on either side of me, we leave the stadium to get some cheese pizza.

CHAPTER 8

Larissa

I 'M SITTING ACROSS THE BOOTH from Easton and P, who insisted she sit next to him, and watching their interaction.

He's been great with her all day. When the pizza, cheese of course, was delivered to our table, she asked him to cut it up for her, and even though I protested that I could do it, he did it himself. All while smiling and listening to my daughter yammer on about how she wants a pink glove but they were sold out when we went to the store.

"Mommy, can I go play games now?" Paisley asks with pizza sauce all over her face.

"Not like that you're not." Easton laughs and gingerly wipes her mouth with a napkin.

Watching him with her pulls at something deep inside me. I've mourned the loss of my husband, but I don't know if I'll ever mourn the loss of the father he was supposed to be to our little girl. I know what it felt like to have his eyes smile at me, what it felt like to be on the receiving end of one of his hugs, but Paisley, she doesn't. Not just Steve, but any man. Now here we sit, with the all-star, the king of the Blaze, Easton Monroe, and he's lavishing her—hell, if I'm honest—both of us with his attention, and my daughter is soaking it up like a sponge. Me, on the other hand, I'm fighting it—this pull I feel every time he ruffles her hair or returns her hug. Every time he smiles down at her then turns that megawatt grin on me, I'm fighting it, but I don't know how much longer I can.

"There," he says, setting down the napkin. "Now can we go, Mom?" he asks. I raise my eyebrows in question, and he shrugs. "We want to play Skee-ball."

"One game, then we need to get going. It's almost your bedtime," I tell her. She nods her little head up and down like a bobblehead doll. Reaching into my purse for some singles, I turn to hand them the money, but they're already gone, racing toward the games.

Just as I'm about to join them, my cell phone rings. When I see Chloe's face on the screen, I know that if I don't answer, she'll keep calling back. "Hey," I greet her, keeping my eyes on Easton and P.

"Where are you?"

"Pizza place just down from the stadium."

"Oh yeah?" she asks coyly. "How was it today? Did you run into him?"

"I did. I saw Drew as well."

"So I heard. I also heard the three of you left together."

"We did."

"And?"

"And what?" I'm evading, and we both know it.

"Spill it, woman."

"He offered to take us to dinner and offered pizza. You know little miss loves her pizza."

"Uh-huh, what next?"

"She was excited, and he's been so good to her all day, I didn't have the heart to tell her no."

"What about you? Has he been good to you?"

"He's... not at all what I pegged him to be. You should see him with her, Chloe. He jumps right in, cutting up her food, wiping her mouth. They're now playing Skee-ball." Once my words register, worry starts to kick in. "What am I doing? I can't let my daughter get attached to him. Stupid," I mutter to myself.

"First of all, it's one day. Second, you're not stupid. You need to open up, live a little. Drew assures me that East is a good guy."

"Said the ax murderer's mother," I bite back.

She laughs. "You know better than that."

She's right, I do. There is just something about him, this feeling I get when he's around that I know deep in my bones he's a good guy. I would never let him get this close to Paisley otherwise. "Still," I try to argue.

"Stop." Chloe whispers something then comes back on the line. "You sound happy, Larissa. For the first time in a long time, I hear hope in your voice. Sure, you risk both of you getting hurt, but life can be painful. That little girl is stronger than what you give her credit for. She's just like her mama."

"I need to go," I say, wanting to go to them.

"Call me later."

"Yeah, let me get P home and in bed." We end the call, and I stand to go find them. What I find has a few more of the bricks around my heart crumbling to the ground. Easton is sitting behind one of those NASCAR driving games with Paisley in his lap, hands clutching the steering wheel.

"Turn to the left," he tells her, laughing as they crash into a wall. "Your other left."

"I don't know which way that is." She giggles. Her laughter is infectious, and I feel a smile spreading across my lips. An outsider looking in would never know that she's not his daughter. They both have dark brown eyes, their hair's an even match for color, and the way he is with her, that alone speaks volumes to me. I stand there and watch them laugh and cut up until the game ends. When Easton climbs out from behind the wheel, Paisley is in his arms, and he places her on his hip. She rests her head on his shoulder, and it takes everything in me not to let the sob that's clogging my throat break free.

"Hey, there's Mommy," he says softly to her.

"You about ready, kiddo? It's been a long day for you," I say, pushing her hair back from her eyes.

"Can East come too?" she asks.

He looks at me, hope brewing in his eyes.

"Maybe another time. We need to get you a bath and into bed."

"You promise?" she asks, pulling at my heartstrings.

Easton reaches out and grabs my hand. "I'll call your mom, and we'll figure out when I can see you again, okay, princess?"

"Okay," she readily agrees with him.

"I'll take her." I hold my arms out.

"I got her. I paid the check, so we should be good to go. Do you have what you need?" he asks me.

"Yes."

He laces his fingers through mine, and that's how we leave the restaurant. At my car, I unlock the door and hold my arms out for P.

"I've got her," he says, setting her in her seat. "Princess, how do you work this thing?" I hear him ask, and she giggles.

"Not like that, East. It goes like this," she explains.

"Are you sure?" His tone is playful.

"Y-yes." She giggles again.

"Thank you for hanging out with me today."

"Thank you too," she says with a yawn.

They mumble a few more words before he stands and shuts the door. He reaches for my hand, and I don't have it in me to pull away. "She's a great kid," he says, his voice low.

"Thank you." I push the words past my lips.

"Can I see the two of you again?" he asks. I must not hide the shocked expression very well, because he continues. "I like you, Larissa. I want to explore that, and she's a part of you, a package deal, the icing on the cake so to speak."

"Not a deal breaker?" I ask him, holding my breath.

"No." His answer is short and firm. "Can I have your number? I'll call you tomorrow, and we can make plans."

I nod, taking his offered phone and typing in my number before handing it back to him. Quickly, his fingers fly across the screen, and I feel my phone vibrate in my purse. "Now you have my number, you know, in case you tossed it in the trash the last time. I want you to use it, Larissa. Call me anytime for any reason."

"Thank you for today. For being so great with her." I don't tell him that the piece of paper that fell out of the menu is tucked away in my wallet. I couldn't seem to make myself throw it away.

"The pleasure was all mine." He steps into me until there is barely any space between us. "I'll call you tomorrow," he says, leaning in and pressing his lips to my forehead. I trample down the disappointment that his lips didn't press to mine. Stepping back, he opens the door for me and waits until I'm inside and driving away before he makes his way to his truck. I watch him in the mirror, sneaking glances until I can no longer see him.

Paisley is asleep by the time we get home, so I carry her in and put her straight to bed. She needs a bath, but tomorrow is Sunday and I don't work until the afternoon. We'll sleep in, make breakfast, and worry about a bath before I drop her off to Mom.

As I'm climbing into bed, my phone pings on the nightstand. Grabbing it, I see an unknown number.

You girls make it
home okay?

Easton.

We did. Miss P fell asleep
on the way home, and
barely moved a muscle
when I carried her to bed.

Easton:

I had a great time with the
two of you. Thank you.

We had fun too.

Easton:

I'll call you tomorrow to
set up plans.

I know you're busy. We
don't expect it. I can handle
breaking it to Paisley.

Easton:

I never break my promises.
Sweet dreams, Ris.

Letting my phone fall to the bed, I close my eyes, and all I see is him. Him with the kids today, him playing with Paisley, them eating pizza and playing arcade games. The way he carried her as if she was precious to him and put her in the car. The way his lips pressed against my forehead. The feel of his hot breath against my skin. I drift off to sleep dreaming of Easton Monroe.

CHAPTER 9
Easton

I T'S BEEN OVER A WEEK since I've seen her. With away games, practice, and team meetings, I've had no time and what time I did have exhaustion set in and my bed was calling my name. This week we have a rare three days in a row without games. I'm hoping out of those three days, I can convince Larissa to go out with me. I know she probably hates to leave Paisley, but I need some time with her. It's selfish, but it's fact. Pulling my phone out of my pocket, I send her a text.

> Hey, Ris. I was hoping you and I could get together soon.

Larissa:

I don't know. I hate to take another night away from Paisley.

> We can bring her if you want.

Larissa:
I don't want to interrupt her routine. She goes to bed early.

> Please?

I wait, tapping the screen of my phone every time it starts to dim, watching for the little bubble to appear that tells me she's responding. Finally, after what feels like a lifetime, the bubble appears and her reply comes through.

Larissa:
I'm off tomorrow night.

> So it's a date?

Larissa:
I'm not sure. I also need to talk to Mum to see if she can watch P.

> We can go early if that helps?

Larissa:
A day date?

> You can call it anything you want as long as I get to spend some time with you.

Larissa:
And P can come too?

She's a cute kid, and of course she's welcome, but I want time with her. I don't say that, because I know as a single mom, her options are limited.

> **Always.**

Larissa:
> Give me some time. I'm wrapping up some homework now.

> **You have class today?**

Larissa:
> I take some online classes, but there are a few I can only take on campus. It's convenient that as long as I log in daily, and submit my work, I'm good to go. Helps that I can do it on days off and after P is in bed.

> **Nice.**

> **So, I'll be waiting to hear from you.**

Larissa:
> Give me fifteen minutes.

> **I'm not going anywhere.**

My words have double meaning, and I know Larissa can figure it out. She's a smart girl. She's more than just her beauty; she's the full package—smart, funny, easygoing, and one hell of a mother. That alone tells me that she's one of the good ones.

That and the fact that she couldn't give a fuck that I'm a major league baseball player. I like that a whole hell of a lot.

Keeping my phone clutched in one hand and the remote in the other, I skim through the channels. Nothing is catching my eye. It's not the lack of options, but the fact that all I can think about is Larissa and if I'm going to get to see her while I'm home. I check my phone knowing damn good and well that I haven't missed a call or text, but on the slight chance, I do it anyway.

What has she done to me?

My phone rings, causing me to jump and fumble the phone. When I get a good grip on it again, I look at the screen and see my little sister Pepper's face. She's ten years younger than me at fifteen. I debate on answering in case Larissa calls, but decide I better. I always tell her she can call me if she doesn't want to call Mom and Dad.

"Hey, Pep," I greet her.

"East, good game yesterday."

"Thanks."

"How are you? It seems like forever since I've talked to you."

"You know how it is during the season. You good?"

"Yeah, just hanging out. I've been babysitting for the Lawrence's down the street. They have five-year-old twins. It's easy money."

I think about Paisley. She's just a year younger and spending all day with her, I'm sure would be an adventure. "That's great. You saving up for a car?" I tease. We all know that Mom and Dad are going to buy her a car, but we all like to tease her that she has to buy it on her own. We were spoiled with Dad being a major league player. Not to the point that we are entitled, but we never wanted for anything either.

"Ha ha, no, just spending money and something to do. Josie went to stay with her grandparents this summer and I'm bored out of my mind."

Her theatrics make me laugh. "Hang in there, kid."

I can practically hear her rolling her eyes at me. "Kid? Really, Easton? I'm fifteen. I'll be sixteen in four months," she reminds me. She reminds all of us daily.

"Sorry, it slipped," I lie.

"Sure," she grumbles. "I better go, I told Mom I would load and unload the dishwasher before she and Dad got home. They'll be here any minute."

"What have you done all day?" I ask her.

"Nothing much, just laid around the pool."

"Go, before you get in trouble. Be good, Pep."

"Love you," she sing-songs, and ends the call.

Just as I'm setting my phone on the table, I get a text notification.

Larissa

I don't want to leave P
with Mom again at night.

Day date?

Luckily tomorrow is a short morning practice. An hour in the weights room and two on the field. I should have plenty of time to still have our day date. If she chooses the morning, I'll make an excuse to Coach, that's how badly I need to see her. To spend some time with her. To see if me missing her is really what this is. What else could it be? She's all I've been able to think about.

Larissa

I don't know.

Please (I'm making
puppy dog eyes at you).

Larissa:

LOL

I'd really love to see you. You name the time.

Larissa:

Noon? Be back by five or so? That way we will be able to have our normal nightly routine.

Noon it is.

Larissa:

Where should we meet?

I can come and pick you up. This is a date.

Larissa:

I would rather meet you.

I always feel as though I'm crashing into a wall with her. They say nothing worth having comes easy; this is a true testament of that.

How about your work? Can you park there?

Larissa:

Yeah, see you then.

I hate that I'm not picking her up, but at this stage in the game, I have to pick and choose my battles. In the grand scheme of things, I've won because she agreed to go out with me. Doesn't matter if it's day or night; I still get to spend time with her.

Now, to plan what we're going to do. I've not really dated much, so this is a whole new ball game for me. No pun intended. I understand she's a widow and that she's doing all of this on her own, I do. However, what she doesn't understand is that I want the chance to get to know her better, to get to know them. Maybe I'm the man who can help her heal? Maybe I'm the man who can be a father figure to Paisley? I've been where they are. I know it's scary as hell. I watched my mom live it. I also watched her give my now father a chance, and our lives are better because of it. Pulling up the search engine on my phone, I type in day date ideas. Desperate times and all that. I don't know if I'll have another chance with her. Up to this point, she's made it difficult. I need to make this date unforgettable.

CHAPTER 10
Larissa

I THOUGHT ABOUT TELLING MOM I had to work a few hours, but decided against it. I knew as soon as I asked her to watch Paisley so I could go on a day date with none other than Tennessee's most eligible bachelor, according to Google. I admit I've done some research. Her grin would be wide and permanent on her face. She's always telling me to go out more, to date, and do things for myself. I always give her the same answer: No one has sparked my interest, and that she and Paisley, well, and Chloe are all the social life I need.

I've been on a few dates since Steven passed, but they're usually double dates with Chloe that never lead to more than dinner and a few drinks.

Maybe I'm broken?

"Go, have fun. No need to rush back," Mom says with Paisley on her hip. "P and I are going to the park, and then I thought we'd bake a cake."

"Yay!" Paisley throws her little arms in the air and cheers.

"I'll be here by five," I say again.

She playfully rolls her eyes. "Well, if things change, don't worry about us. In fact, I was hoping for a sleepover."

"Can I Momma, please, please?" Paisley begs.

"Mom, you keep her so much."

"Of course, I do. That's what grandmothers are for. Go, we've got this. You have fun, live a little. Take all the time you need. I'll see you tomorrow morning for breakfast."

"I have to be at work at ten."

"Then you better get up and get moving, lazy bones," she laughs, and Paisley mimics her, throwing her head back in laughter. "I'll have pancakes and bacon ready at nine."

"Thanks, Mom." I lean in and give them both a hug, kissing P on the cheek. "You be good for Gram."

"Mommy, I'm always good," she says dramatically.

My baby girl is four going on fourteen. "You girls behave," I say with a final wave as I rush out the door. The entire drive to The Vineyard, I try not to think about today, about this date I've agreed to. He's so damn hard to keep resisting.

Pulling into the lot, I see him in his truck. He hops out and rushes to my door, opening it for me. "Hey, Ris." He leans in and kisses my cheek.

"Hi," I say awkwardly. I feel like a giddy teenager when I'm with him. I need to get that in check. I'm a grown woman, a mother. He's just another guy. I need to not let his job, his fame, intimidate me.

"You ready?" he asks.

"Sure, what are we doing?"

"I thought about today a lot and decided I wanted to share something that I love with you."

"Oh," I say, because what do you say to that? Easton Monroe is not at all what I expected. He continues to surprise me.

"Yeah, then I thought we could grab a bite to eat. I know you need to be back by five, so I hope I have it all planned out okay."

I feel a little guilty about the deadline. When I told him five o'clock, it was so I could keep my daughter in her routine. Well, and to keep my distance from him. He's sexy and charming, and I need all the help I can get. "That sounds good," I finally say. What I should tell him is there is no time limit, but I can't seem to push the words past my lips.

The ride is filled with casual conversation. Easton asks me about school and my job. "So yeah, I have just two semesters to go," I tell him.

"That's great. You should be proud of everything you've accomplished while working and raising your daughter."

"You do what you have to do."

He nods. "How is she, Princess Paisley?"

I smile at the sweet name he's given her. "Right now, she's in heaven. She's staying with my mom. They're going to the park and then baking a cake."

He laughs. "Uh oh, you think she'll be hyped up on sugar when you pick her up?"

I hesitate for just a few seconds before I answer him. "Actually, when I dropped her off, Mom insisted she keep her overnight. I hate asking her to do so because she does it so much when I work the evening shift. She was adamant that I live a little. Her words, not mine," I confess.

He reaches over and gives my hand a gentle squeeze. "So I have you for more than a few hours?" His voice is hopeful.

I bite on my bottom lip and take a deep breath. "I think we should just see how things go."

With a quick glance in my direction, he gives me his crooked grin. I'm glad I'm sitting because the effects would have surely made my knees weak. "Challenge accepted."

Shaking my head, I fight my smile. Like I said, charming.

"We're here," he says, pulling into a parking lot.

"Where is here?" I ask him. The building is unmarked.

"You'll see." He grins. Grabbing his keys, he hops out of the truck and rushes around to open my door. As soon as I'm on solid ground, he laces his fingers through mine and places his phone to his ear with his free hand. "Hey, Larry, yeah, just pulled up. Great, thanks," he says, ending the call.

"A hint?" I ask. He's obviously planned this out since he's let someone know we've arrived.

"You'll see soon enough." He walks us to a side entrance door and knocks three times. Not a minute later, an older gentleman wearing a uniform, the name *Larry* on the chest, is opening the door and ushering us in. "Good to see you," Easton says, holding out his hand for the older man to shake.

"You too, E. Everything's all set up. Take your time. I'm working on the floors in the locker room," he tells him.

"Thanks," Easton replies. "You ready?"

"For?" I ask again.

"Batting cages." He grins. Again. I swear his grin is so wide and so bright, I could see it from my front porch.

"I've never been to the batting cages."

"Perfect. I can show you." With my hand still encased in his, he leads us down a hall and through a set of double doors.

"Batting cages?" I ask when I see what's in front of us.

"Yeah." He gives my hand a gentle squeeze. "I wanted to share a part of who I am with you. Not Easton the major leaguer, but Easton the guy who grew up loving the sport. The guy who spent more time at the batting cages than he did anywhere else. I also thought that if Paisley ended up coming with us, she would have fun too."

"You were serious?" I ask. I thought he was just being nice saying that P could tag along.

"Of course I was. She's a part of you, Larissa."

"I just thought—"

He cuts me off. "You just thought what? That I wanted to sleep with you and this was my way of getting that? I've already told you that's not what this is about. What do I have to do to make you believe me?"

"I'm sorry," I say immediately. "I shouldn't have assumed or judged you." I look around the room and see we're the only ones here. "Is this place closed?"

"It is. I called in a favor. I didn't want people pointing their cell phones at us all night. I'm used to it, but I know you aren't and if Paisley were here, I didn't want them to get shots of her and for her to end up in the papers too."

"Thank you." I'm grateful he put so much thought into this. For me and my daughter. "So, this is a first for me, Monroe. You're going to have to show me how it's done." I bat my eyelashes at him like a damn fool. I can feel my face heat from embarrassment. I'm terrible at flirting, at dating.

His eyes darken. "I got you," he says, pulling me into him. My back is aligned with his front. His lips are next to my ear when he whispers, "I've got moves," he says huskily.

I shiver, not quite sure if it's from his hot breath or the words, and the meaning behind them. His hands land on my hips and he turns me slightly to the right. Apparently, my prior embarrassment, although felt foolish, did the trick.

"Now, stand like this," he instructs.

"Oh, *those* kinds of moves," I say once I find my voice.

"Larissa!" he mock scolds. "You have a dirty mind. I would never." He smirks when I look at him.

"Uh-huh, let's get on with the shot, Mr. I've-got-moves."

"What?" he asks innocently. "I do. I'd be happy to show them to you. All of them."

I can't help but laugh when he winks at me. "Show me what to do." His eyes darken, and I have to admit I'm turned on. It's been a long time since I've actually enjoyed a man's company, and felt any kind of attraction.

"Okay, let's start like this." For the next two hours, we hit ball after ball. Easton positions me, stands behind me, and even hits a few with me. My body is... alive and already craves his touch. I might have even pretended I forgot what he told me a time or two, just so he would stand behind me and wrap his arms around me again.

I'm hitting round after round, and I have to admit now that I'm making contact, I'm enjoying this more than I thought I would. P would have loved it.

Easton steps back and tells me it's my turn again. I step up to the plate and get into my stance. Holding up my bat, I give him a nod that I'm ready to go. I feel more confident this round. When the ball is released, I remember what he's shown me. I wait until what I feel like is the right moment and swing the bat. Not only does it connect, but it also flies through the air to the back of the net. It's my best hit yet. I drop the bat and jump up and down. "Yes!" I cheer.

Easton rushes to me and picks me up, swinging me around. Then he starts to sing "Girl on Fire" by Alicia Keys, causing me to burst out laughing.

"Don't quit your day job," I tease.

"It's true. The more you hit, the better you're getting. I'm impressed," he says, setting me back on my feet.

I pretend to brush something off my shoulder. "You know, all in a day's work."

"You had enough?" he asks, laughing.

"Yeah," I say, even though I'm not ready for our time to end.

He grins. "On to the next adventure."

"What might that be?" I try to hide my smile but fail. I'm having a great time and am glad I didn't let my worries or fear keep me from our day date.

"It's a surprise." He kisses the tip of my nose. After lacing his fingers through mine, we say goodbye to Larry before we're back on the road.

CHAPTER 11
Easton

P LANNING DATES IS NOT MY thing. Planning dates that an adorable four-year-old might be tagging along with is challenging. I wanted to spend time with Larissa, and Paisley if she had been with us, but I wanted them both to have fun and feel comfortable. So I planned a picnic. At first I was going to go to the park, but not wanting them to end up on the front page of the tabloids, I decided to call in a favor. Tank Thomas played with my dad, and to this day, they remain good friends. He owns a large farm not far from here. Thankfully, he said we could stay as long as we liked. He and his wife are out of town. It's the perfect spot with lots of privacy. I ordered food from a local deli, packed up a couple of old blankets, a cooler for water, and I threw in a couple of juice boxes for Paisley just in case.

Kids drink juice, right?

I also picked up a Frisbee, and I found a new pink glove, the smallest I could find. I got Larissa one too so the three of us could play catch. Not sure Larissa will want to play catch, but lying back on the blanket with her, just talking sounds pretty damn good to me. She's unlike anyone I've ever met. So far, today has been perfect.

"I just need to make a quick stop," I tell her. I want to reach over and hold her hand or set mine on her warm thigh, but I keep both hands on the wheel. The last thing I need is to scare her away because I can't keep my hands off her.

"That's fine. I'm with you." She smiles. As the day goes on, those smiles seem to come easier for her. I have to fight the urge to puff my chest out, pretty sure I'm the reason behind her smiles. I'm doing that. Making her smile. She has a lot on her plate with working, school, and Paisley. I'm glad today I could give her a day of fun. A day to maybe not think about all her responsibilities. Larissa takes care of everyone, that much is already obvious, and dammit if I don't want to be the one to take care of her. This connection we have is real. I feel it with every touch, every look. I'm out of my element with her, but I'll be damned if I let that scare me away.

The stop at the deli is quick. Everything packed up in a wicker picnic basket like I requested. I didn't care what it cost; I wanted today to be special.

"Look at you," Larissa says when I place the basket in the back seat.

"What?" I feign innocence.

"Let me guess, boy scout?" she teases.

I throw my head back and laugh. "Just like to be prepared." The place we're going to is about twenty minutes outside of town.

"Where are you taking me, Monroe?" she asks.

"Take a guess?"

"By the looks of things, a picnic?"

"Yep. You good with that?"

"No complaints." Her mouth tilts into a warm smile as she settles back in her seat. We make idle chitchat. She teases me about my planning, and I take every bit of it. I love seeing her carefree and smiling. "Who lives here?" she asks when I pull into the driveway.

"A good friend of the family."

"Do they care that we're here? Going to jail is not on my to-do list," she says with a hint of a smile in her voice.

"No jail, at least not today," I say, causing her mouth to drop open. I throw my head back and laugh. "Relax, Ris. I'm trying to get you to want to spend time with me, that's a sure-fire way to make sure that never happens."

"As long as we're on the same page." She winks and climbs out of the truck. "What can I carry?" she asks.

"Grab that bag," I say, pointing to the backpack I brought with the gloves, balls, and Frisbee. I gather the basket, throw the small cooler strap over my shoulder, and grab both blankets. "This way, madam." I bow my head to her, causing her laughter to flow freely once again. That's a sound I would love to hear every day. I lead us behind the house and to the garage. Tank gave me the security code so we could use the golf cart to get back to the pond and gazebo.

"Seriously, Easton. You do know these people, right?" she asks, worrying her bottom lip.

Leaning in, I press a kiss to her cheek then whisper in her ear, "Yes, I know these people. No way would I risk losing you when I finally have your attention." Pulling away, I load the blankets, basket, cooler, and bag of supplies onto the golf cart. "Hop on," I tell her. She doesn't hesitate, and the smile on her face tells me she's excited for what's to come.

I drive us down to the pond and stop just at the edge of the dock. Quickly, we unload, and I begin to make a spot for use. Once I have the blankets spread out, the basket and the cooler all set up, we settle in for lunch.

"This is really nice," she says, popping a grape in her mouth.

"It's quiet here, and I wasn't sure if Paisley was coming. I thought she could run and play. I also brought two blankets in case she wanted to nap."

"She's opposed to those these days. Even when she does take them, they're short." A blush touches her cheeks. "Sorry."

"For what?" I ask, reaching out and tucking a loose strand of hair behind her ear.

"I'm sure you don't want to hear me babble on about my daughter's napping habits."

"Is she a part of you?"

She looks over at me, her expression confused. "She's the best part of me."

"Then I want to hear you talk about her. She's your life, Larissa. I get that. All I'm asking is a chance to be a part of that as well."

She's quiet for several long minutes staring off in the distance. "You don't make it easy on a girl, do you?"

"Nothing worth having comes easy," I say.

"What's in the bag?" she asks, changing the subject.

"This is me trying to be prepared." Reaching for the bag, I unzip it and pull out the Frisbee. "You can't come to a place like this with wide-open spaces without a Frisbee."

"I think it's a law," she teases.

Delving into the bag once more, I pull out the small pink glove. "Found this," I say, handing it to her.

She takes the glove and turns it over in her hands. "You remembered." She looks up at me, and her smile is blinding.

"Of course I did. Princess P wanted a pink glove, but they didn't have one in her size."

"I don't know what to say."

"Don't say anything. Just listen." Setting the bag aside, I reach for her hand, holding it in mine. I softly trace her knuckles with my thumb and wait for her to look at me. When she does, I let the words tumble free. "I like you, Larissa. I'm not playing games. I know you're a single mom and that Paisley is, as she should be, the most important person in your world. I just want the chance to be a part of that world. To spend time with you, and her. To get to know you and see if this electricity I feel every time I'm with you is what I imagine it to be."

She closes her eyes and nods. I don't say anything else, giving her time to process what I'm saying. When her eyes open, they say so much. She wants to trust me, but she's guarded. I don't care how long it takes, I'll earn that trust from her. From both of them. I can feel her fear, her reluctance pouring off her. Is it that she's still mourning the loss of her husband? Is it the fact that my life is in the spotlight? Maybe she's fearful of losing yet another important person in her life? Whatever those fears may be, I want to demolish them. I want her to smile like she was just moments ago. I want her laughter. I want to watch her be the incredible mother I already know she is. Whatever she's hiding behind those walls, I want to be the man to knock them down.

"What else is in the bag?" she asks after clearing her throat.

Not letting go of her hand, I reach again for the bag with my other. I pull out two more gloves and a couple of balls. "We couldn't give her the pink glove she's always wanted and not use it." I wink.

"You thought of everything." She smiles. It's softer than those I received earlier, but I'll take it. Never would I turn down one of her beautiful smiles.

"Maybe I always wanted to be a boy scout," I say, and her smile grows. "Let's eat." I remove the fresh fruit, pretzels, and sandwiches from the picnic basket. "We have turkey clubs, a plain turkey, and a plain cheese. I wasn't sure what Paisley would eat, but I know she loves her cheese."

"That she does. That was very thoughtful of you, Easton. Thank you for going out of your way, just on the idea that she might be with us today."

"So how did I do?" I ask. "Cheese or plain turkey for the princess?"

"She would have either, but she would have chosen the cheese."

"Yes." I throw my hands up in the air celebrating my victory. "What about you?"

"Turkey club is perfect."

"That's two for two," I say, holding up two fingers.

"Gloating, Mr. Monroe?"

"Celebrating. There's a difference."

"Uh-huh," she laughs.

We spend a couple of hours lying on the blankets talking. She tells me stories about Paisley, and I tell her stories about growing up as an older brother. Sometimes we just sit in silence, hands linked, staring up at the sky. It's simple, yet perfect. This is one of the best days I can ever remember having.

"I know it's getting close to five, but I'm not ready for today to end."

"It's been a good day," she agrees.

"How about dinner?"

"I really should be getting home. I have a ton of assignments I need to get caught up on, and with P being at Mom's, it's a great time to do it."

I'm disappointed, but I understand. She has no time for herself; it's all work, school, and her daughter. I'm in awe of her. "Let's get packed up and get you back to your car." We make quick work of packing up, and we're on our way in no time.

"Thank you, Easton," she says once I pull my truck up next to her SUV. "I didn't know what to expect today, but this... thank you."

"We should have day dates more often." I smile over at her.

"Yeah, maybe we should." With that, she climbs out of the truck. I hurry to do the same and walk with her to the driver's side of her SUV.

"Can I call you later?" I ask.

"We just spent the majority of the day together."

"And it's still not enough," I say, stepping in closer.

I watch as she swallows, the column of her throat sexy as hell. "Yeah, that would be fine."

"Thank you for agreeing to see me today, Larissa. I can't remember a day that I've enjoyed more." Leaning in, I kiss the corner of her mouth. "Drive safe." With that, I step back and open her door. I stand there until she drives away, watching until I can no longer see her.

I really like this girl.

CHAPTER 12
Larissa

I'VE BEEN SITTING ON THE couch with my laptop for the last four hours. My eyes are tired, and my stomach just growled.

I'm feeling pretty good about where I am with my classes. It's been a productive evening. I refused to think about Easton, pushing him out of my mind. If not, I knew I'd get nothing done. Now here I am at almost ten in the evening, and my studying is not only caught up, but I'm ahead. I don't know that I've ever been ahead before. I shut down my laptop and stack my binder and notebooks on the end table when my phone rings.

Easton.

I take a deep breath to tamp down the excitement of seeing his name on my screen. I'm acting like a teenager, but I can't seem to control it where he's concerned. "Hello," I answer.

"Hey, Ris. How's studying going?" The deep timbre of his voice washes over me. It's soothing.

"Good. I'm actually caught up and worked a little ahead. I just put it all away for the night. My eyes are going crossed. I've stared at my computer screen long enough."

"That's good to hear. Have you eaten?"

"Not yet. I was actually just going to head to the kitchen and see what I could find."

"I could bring you something."

"That's sweet of you, but I can just find something here."

"You sure?"

"I'm sure. How was the rest of your day?" I ask, opening the freezer door. I spot one of the single serve microwave pizzas that P loves and grab it. As quietly as I can, I open the package and place it in the microwave. I don't want to miss a word he has to say.

"Uneventful. I came home, did some laundry, worked out a little, then went for a swim."

"Ah, the life of a professional athlete," I tease.

"More like the life of a man who's trying really fucking hard not to end up on your doorstep tonight."

"Oh really?" I ask. I keep my voice calm, but on the inside, I have that feeling, the one that starts in the pit of your stomach and then washed over you. It's a feeling of longing and want.

"I miss you already. I can't stop thinking about you, and I know you're home alone. If it weren't for the fact that I know you not only need but deserve this free time to get caught up, I'd be pounding down your door."

"It's been nice. Don't get me wrong. I love my daughter, but to actually be caught up and be a little bit ahead of schedule, it feels good. I have to admit."

"Then my suffering was worth it," he says dramatically.

"Listen to you," I say with a laugh. The microwave beeps, and it's loud. "Sorry, that's my dinner," I say.

"What are you having?"

"A frozen microwave pizza."

"Sounds... delicious?" he asks.

"P loves them. They're quick and easy. I keep them on hand for those days when cooking just isn't in the cards. I try to keep her on a balanced diet, so I usually cut up some fruit or open a can of vegetables to go with it."

"I bet she loves that." Amusement laces his words.

"The fruit yes, the vegetables not so much. Not unless it's peas. The kid loves peas, which is odd."

"That is kind of odd," he chuckles. "How is she?"

"Paisley? She's living it up at Mom's. I called to check on her, and they were baking a cake. I'm going over there to have breakfast with them in the morning before work. I have to work the early shift."

"I have to be at the stadium at six for team lifting, but then I'm done for the day."

"Plans?" I ask, a little surprised at how easy it is to chat with him.

"Not really. There's this girl I met." My heart picks up speed at his words. "She works at a pretty nice restaurant. I might swing by for lunch."

"You seem to be putting forth a lot of effort for this girl."

"She's worth it."

That feeling washes over me again. "I guess I should let you go then. You know, since you have to get up so early."

"Are you going to bed?" he asks.

"Not yet. I'll probably do a couple of loads of laundry before crashing."

"Mind if I keep you company?" he asks.

His request should startle me, but it doesn't. "Easton, it's late—"

He cuts me off. "Just on the phone, Ris."

"That's a pretty long phone conversation."

"I need to know more about you," he counters.

"Yeah? Like what?" I'm smiling so big my face might crack. He's persistent, and I find it harder and harder to keep pushing him away. He's so easy to talk to and to be around. Today was a true testament of that.

"Like your favorite flavor of ice cream... how old were you when you had your first kiss, among other things," he says, his voice low and husky.

"Are we there yet?" I tease, awareness traveling through me.

"I am. I don't know if you are, but I sure as hell am."

I don't hold back my grin. "You go first," I say. That's how our night goes. Over the next two hours, we talk about movies, and music, and food. Nothing too heavy, just small mundane things getting to know each other. I've managed to wash, dry, and fold two loads of laundry, and now I'm ready to crash. "It's almost one in the morning. We both have to get up early. You earlier than me."

"I know."

"We should probably get some sleep."

"Thank you for today, and for tonight."

"Shouldn't I be the one thanking you?"

He laughs. "I mean, I am Easton Monroe."

"Hush. Get some sleep, slugger," I say.

"Night, Ris. Sweet dreams."

Night." I end the call, plug my phone that is almost dead into the charger, and crawl under the covers. As I drift off to sleep, it's his smile that I see, and his touch that I feel as if he were here with me.

Sweet dreams indeed.

CHAPTER 13
Easton

I'VE BEEN DRIVING MYSELF CRAZY all morning trying to think of something fun I can do with Larissa and Paisley. I want to make a good impression, and everything I come up with seems lame. Grabbing my phone to call Mom and ask her opinion—desperate times and all that—I notice I have an e-mail from the Blaze management. Scrolling through, I see it's a reminder that the Blaze family day is at the zoo this Saturday. If I'm interested in attending, I need to give them the number of attendees so they can prepare my passes.

Someone is watching over me.

Quickly, I reply that I need three tickets, two adults and one child. I had forgotten all about the event and wasn't even sure I was going to go. A single guy at the zoo isn't much fun. A single guy, the girl he wants to get to know, and her adorable daughter... that sounds a hell of a lot more appealing. Instead of calling Mom, I call Larissa.

"Hello," she answers, and her voice is gruff from sleep. Looking at the clock, I see it's just after eight in the morning.

"Did I wake you?" I ask, trying not to think about her all snuggled up in her bed.

"I was just lying here. P woke me up about ten minutes ago."

"She's an early riser?"

"Pretty much."

"Who is it, Momma?" I hear her sweet, angelic voice ask.

She hesitates. "It's Easton."

"I wanna say hi." There is a rustle with the phone. Then I hear, "Hey, East, whatcha doing?"

"Morning, princess. I was just calling your mom to plan for us to spend the day together next Saturday." I know it's a dick move to get Paisley excited before I run it past Larissa, but I'm hoping that works in my favor. I can't have her backing out on me.

"Are we gonna play catch?" she asks.

"Nope, but I need to ask your mommy first. Can you hand her back the phone?"

"Mommy, Easton wants to talk to you."

"Hey," Larissa says, and I can hear the smile in her voice.

"So, I have this thing on Saturday, and I was wondering if you and Paisley would come with me?"

"What kind of thing?" she asks cautiously.

"The Blaze are having a team family day at the zoo. They close the place down for us, and we pretty much have free rein. I thought Paisley would enjoy it."

"She'll love it," she admits. "What time?"

I throw my fist in the air in silent celebration. "I'll pick you ladies up at eleven."

"Okay," she whispers.

"Okay," I repeat. "Great. Send me your address."

"I can do that. I have to get moving and make breakfast. Then I have to work this afternoon."

"Just when you have time. Have a good night at work."

"Thanks, Easton. I'll talk to you soon."

"Bye, East!" Paisley yells as the line goes dead.

I can't wipe the smile off my face. I spend the rest of the day lounging and getting caught up on things around the house. We have two home games this week, hence the reason for the team day at the zoo on Saturday.

By nightfall, I find myself sitting on the back deck, untouched bottle of beer sitting on the table. I was antsy in the house, pacing, not sure what to do with myself. That's not something I'm used to. I was tempted to go to The Vineyard for dinner but didn't want to push my luck. Now here I am wishing I had gone, while cursing myself inwardly for not doing so.

Pushing the home button on my cell phone, I see it's a little after ten. I'm not sure what time she gets off work tonight, but the last time it was eleven. I'm in the house, locking the patio door, grabbing my keys, and heading to the garage before I can talk myself out of it.

The closer I get to the restaurant, the calmer I become. The antsy feeling slips away completely when I pull into the parking lot. The spot next to her Escape is open. Just like last time, I take a seat on the tailgate of my truck and wait for her.

I check the time what seems like every thirty seconds. I realize she might get out later than eleven, but I'm hoping that's not the case. Three minutes after eleven, the back door opens, and I lay eyes on her for the first time today.

"Easton?" she asks cautiously.

"Hey, Ris," I say, not moving. I want to though. I want to hop off this tailgate, pull her into my arms, and kiss the ever-loving fuck out of her. Instead, I stay rooted to my spot.

"What are you doing here?" she asks, stopping just in front of me. She's no longer in her uniform. Instead, she's wearing jeans, with holes in the knees and a tank top.

"I wanted to see you," I tell her honestly. I don't want to play games, not with her.

"You were with me most of the day yesterday," she reminds me, even though she doesn't need to. I've replayed our day together over and over.

"Yeah, and today, nothing. I needed my Larissa fix."

A slight tilt of her lip appears and disappears just as quickly. She's trying to hide it, but it was there. "Where's Paisley?" I ask her.

"She's staying at my mom's tonight."

"So you have nowhere to be? You going somewhere," I ask. I'm not used to her coming out dressed in something other than her uniform.

She hesitates. "No, not really."

"Why the change of clothes?" I ask, knowing it's not really any of my business. But the thought of her possibly meeting up with someone else lights a fire inside me.

"Oh, I was running late, so I changed here. My last table was a family and the kid, a little older than P, was rushing back from the bathroom and ran into me. A full plate of spaghetti and meatballs right down my shirt. Luckily I had clothes with me so I changed after we closed up."

I breathe a sigh of relief. "Have you eaten?"

"Yeah, one of the perks of the job."

"You wanna go for a drink or maybe just a drive?" I'm reaching, and we both know it. I just want to spend some time with her. Hell, we can sit here in this parking lot and just talk if that gets me time with her.

"A drive?" She poses it as a question.

I jump off the tailgate and close it. Reaching for her hand, I guide her to the passenger door and open it for her. I wait for her to get situated before closing her door and rushing to the other side. I slide in behind the wheel and look over at her. "You look good in that seat," I tell her.

She smiles. "Yeah, the leather really sets the backdrop."

"You're beautiful, Larissa. You don't need a backdrop." She swallows hard, and I want to lean over and kiss the column of her neck. Instead, I start the truck and pull out of the lot.

"So, where are we going?" she asks.

"I have an idea." I'm evasive in my answer. I want to take her to my house, but I know we're not there yet. Instead, I'm taking her to my second home. The drive is quiet, but not uncomfortably so.

"We're going to the stadium?" she asks as we pull into the lot.

"We are. I wanted to share this with you." She doesn't say anything to that, not that I expected her to. Larissa analyzes everything. She just needs a little time to catch up to where I am. At the moment, I want nothing more than to spend as much time with her and her daughter as possible. I was raised with the mindset that family is everything. I grew up watching my uncles, my dad's brothers, fall hard and fast with the loves of their lives, and it's as if a light is switched on. The light is on and shining brightly down on Larissa.

Parking my truck in my reserved spot, I climb out and rush to her door.

"You sure we're allowed to be here?" She glances around the empty parking lot.

"I'm sure." Taking her hand in mine, I lead her to the players' entrance gate. Pulling out my key, I make quick work of unlocking the gate and pulling her through.

"You have a key?"

"I do." I grin. I don't tell her that I had to come back last week to get my gear that I left and had to swing by coach's house to get his extra key and have yet to give it back. Making sure the gate is secure behind us, I lead her down the dimly lit hallway. Her hand clutches onto mine. On instinct, I release her hand and place my arm over her shoulders, holding her next to me.

"It's so quiet," she says in awe.

"Yeah, it's a lot different after hours." I lead her out onto the field that's lit only from the lights of the surrounding city and the night sky. I don't stop until we reach the outfield.

"Wow," she whispers, looking up at the stars.

Her head is tilted toward the night sky, and her hair is cascading down her back. I step close, invading her space. When she lifts her head, our eyes collide and our breaths mingle. "You're beautiful, Larissa." My hand reaches up to cup her cheek. Her hand grips my wrist, and I hesitate just long enough for her to push me away. She doesn't. Closing the space between us, I press my lips to hers. I have to fight to keep it slow, to not devour her.

"East," she whimpers.

"Yeah, baby?"

"What are we doing?"

"I'm kissing you." I trail my lips down her jaw.

"But why?"

"Because I can't not kiss you," I say, kissing her just below her ear before pulling away. Sitting down in the middle of the outfield, I tug on her hand and motion for her to sit between my legs. She hesitates but eventually takes her place nestled between my thighs, her back to my chest. Immediately, I wrap my arms around her and bury my face in her neck. "Tell me what I have to do?"

"What do you mean?"

"What do I have to do for you to give us... give this a chance?"

"Why me?"

"Besides the fact that my body prickles with awareness anytime you're near? How about the fact that you're not impressed with my career or the fact that I'm a Monroe? You make me work for your attention. I haven't stopped thinking about you since the day I met you."

"I'm a single mom, busting my ass to make ends meet. You don't need that baggage."

"Can I tell you a story?"

"Yeah," she whispers.

"One day there was this ten-year-old little boy name Easton. His father was a bad guy, a crooked cop, heavy into drugs who no longer wanted his family. Easton and his mom started over on their own. They were doing fine on their own, but one day that all changed. A man, a good man, fell in love with his mother, fell in love with him. That man changed their lives for the better. He loved them both as if they'd always been his. He brought them a family—brothers, sisters, uncles, aunts, cousins, and grandparents. Suddenly Easton and his mom were more than doing fine. They were great."

"Is that true?"

"Yeah, my dad, he adopted me after he and my mom got married. He's never once treated me as if I'm not his biological son. His family welcomed me and my mom with open arms." I tighten my hold on her. "That little girl is a part of you, Larissa. I know this is a package deal. I wouldn't pursue this otherwise."

"Your father is a good man."

"The best," I say, before kissing the top of her head. "I know this is all fast, but I've never wanted someone the way I want you. Not just so I can fuck you." She tenses in my arms, and I rush to finish what I was saying. "It's more than that. I just like being around you. Your smile lights me up inside. And as far as your little princess, she's just that, an adorable little girl who I would be honored to get to spend more time with."

"I'm worried she's going to get attached to you and she's going to get her heart broken." A pang of longing hits me, causing an ache deep in my chest. I want her to get attached to me. I want to be engrained in their lives. I know I have to prove it to her, but no way would I break either of their hearts. In fact, it would be quite the opposite if she were to let me in and then push me back out of their lives. My heart would be the one broken.

"I won't hurt either of you. I know what's at stake here. I know it's more than just about me and how much I want you. I know what it means to date a single mom; I've lived it."

"Yet you're still here."

"I'm still here. This is where I want to be." Her body relaxes against me, and I smile in silent victory that maybe, just maybe, I'm getting through to her. "Tell me about her dad."

Rather than stiffening in my arms like I expected her to at the mention of her husband, I'm relieved when she presses even closer to me. "Steve and I were high school sweethearts. We had everything all planned out. We'd both work and save up money. He would go to the police academy first since it was a shorter program. Once he got a full-time job, I'd start on my degree. We were so young and a lot alike. He was a foster kid, and well, all I had was my mom. The day we found out I was pregnant, we were thrilled but scared out of our minds. He left for work that same morning, and I never saw him again. A few hours later, there was a uniformed officer at our front door telling me he was killed in the line of duty."

"I don't know what to say to that," I confess. Although it would mean we were not here in this moment, I wish I could somehow change the outcome for her. For both of them. Then it hits me. I can change it now. Maybe that's why I met her, maybe that's the pull I feel toward them.

"Yeah, I get that a lot. Steve had life insurance, but it was small. We were young and thought we had time. He was a rookie so his pension and benefits, although helpful, weren't much. It was enough to cover the funeral and get caught up on the bills I was behind on from not being able to... function for a few weeks after his death. Eventually, I knew I had to start living again, for our baby. I gave her his middle name, Paisley Gray. I wanted her to always know she had that part of him. I don't know what I would have done without my mom. She's helped me so much, watching her on days she doesn't have to work."

"What about the other times?"

"She goes to daycare."

"Damn, Ris," I murmur into her neck. Our stories are so similar yet so very different. I can't help but think that if she would let me in, if this thing building between us grows even more, she wouldn't have to work. She could focus on finishing school and taking care of P. Hell, I would do that for her now. That's how important these two have become to me.

"What?"

"I know this is going to sound bad, but hearing what you've been through, how strong you are, it makes me even more attracted to you. You're a fighter. It takes a strong woman to be with a professional athlete. You remind me a lot of my mom, in a non-creepy way." I laugh. "She did what she had to do to make ends meet, working two jobs. I admire you for that."

"Thank you," she says, looking over her shoulder at me. Her eyes shine in the moonlight. They captivate me, but it's the look itself that leaves me speechless.

Acceptance.

I can see it. She's no longer hiding. I know I still have a long way to go, but this feels like a huge victory. Leaning in, I press my lips to hers, and as I trace her lips with my tongue, she opens for me. I'm not sure how we manage it without breaking the kiss, but she turns to face me, straddling my thighs. My hands grip her ass, guiding her so that she's rubbing her pussy over my hard cock.

"Oh God," she moans.

"You like that, baby?" I ask against her lips.

"It's been so long," she murmurs.

"How long?" Her eyes are closed, and her teeth are sunk into her bottom lip. I cup her face in my hands. "Larissa, how long?"

Her eyes pop open. "Since Steve. There's been no one since him."

"Clarify that for me, babe. No one... as in... no one has been inside you?" I thrust my cock against her for good measure. "Has anyone had their mouth here?" I ask, bringing my hand around and tweaking her nipple through her thin cotton shirt.

Eyes locked on mine, she humbles me with her words. "No one has touched me or even kissed me since him. It's just been you."

My lips crash against hers, my hands finding their way back to her ass and gripping her tightly. Together, we rock her hips back and forth over my hard cock. Her head is tilted back, and her eyes are tightly closed. The moonlight shines down on us, and I commit this to memory—the way she looks bathed in the moonlight, writhing against my cock.

"Don't stop," she moans when I loosen my grip, taking in her beauty.

"I've got you, babe." I grip her ass, lift my hips, and guide her back and forth, over and over again.

"I...." She moans deep in the back of her throat.

"Come for me, Ris. Let me have it, baby. I've got you. Let go," I coax her.

Her hands clamp down on my shoulders as she rides me. "Oh God, Easton!" She shouts out my name, and it takes everything I have not to blow my load in my pants like a teenager.

She slumps against me, and I take the opportunity to wrap my arms around her. She returns my embrace as if I'm her lifeline. What she doesn't realize is that I want to be exactly that. Breaking our embrace, I cup her face in my hands and kiss her lips, then her chin. "I think that gives a new meaning to a home run," I tease. Her laughter echoes throughout the stadium.

My cock is still in my pants, hard as steel, twitching and wanting more of her. This still qualifies as the hottest sexual experience of my life. Tonight just solidifies what I already knew: I'm in deep with this girl.

Time to bring my A game.

CHAPTER 14
Larissa

I HAVEN'T SEEN EASTON SINCE that night at the stadium. His schedule has been grueling with practices and two games this week. Mine has been just as crazy with work, class, and Paisley. He's texted and called every day. He even tried to convince me to bring P to a game, but I declined. She's talked about today all week. She loves the zoo, and she's pretty fond of Easton too. I like to keep her on as much of a routine as I can, so a late-night game just wasn't in the cards. Easton made me promise that his next weekend home game we would come. I caved. Of course I did. I can't seem to tell him no. Not that I really want to. Something changed between us that night at the stadium. I still worry that this is all going to end in disaster. It's not so much the heartache. P and I can get through that. It's the thought of giving him all of me, and losing him. Not just breaking up, but something terrible happening to him. I could live with us not being together. I could handle that pain, so could P. We would have to. But truly losing him, not breathing the same air as him, that's a fear I'm struggling with. After losing my father and then Steven.... Tragedy takes the men that I love, but there is something about him, his smile, or the way he treats me, and let's not forget the way he is with Paisley. I can't resist him. I just hope and pray it all works out in the end.

"Mommy, when will he be here?" Paisley says from her perch in the window. She's been staring outside for the last twenty minutes.

"He should be here any minute." I barely have the words out of my mouth when she screams "Easton!" and runs to the front door.

"Don't open that door, missy," I yell after her.

"But it's East." She says it like he's her best friend—then again, in her four-year-old mind, he just might be.

"Regardless of who you think it is, you never open the door without an adult with you. Understood?"

"Yeah, can we open the door now," she says, dismissing me with her little diva attitude. It comes out every now and then, and I know today it's because she can hardly contain her excitement. When he knocks on the door, she yells his name excitedly yet again. I pull the door open, and she launches herself at him. "East, I didn't think you would ever come get me."

He laughs, catching her in his arms. "How could I ever forget about Princess Paisley?" he asks sweetly. I can see her melt under his affection. Sad thing is, I do the same damn thing. "I have something for you." He hands her a small pink gift bag, setting her back on her feet. Leaning against the door, I watch them.

"A pink glove!" She launches herself at him for the second time in a matter of minutes. "Oh, thank you, thank you, thank you. I so so love it. It's beautiful. A princess glove."

"For a princess," he beams his megawatt smile at her.

"Hey, Ris." He pulls his attention from her and smiles at me. "You ladies ready to go?"

"Yeah, let me grab my bag." I reach for my small Under Armour backpack.

"What's in the bag?" he questions.

"Supplies. Baby wipes, a change of clothes, snacks, and a couple of bottles of water."

"Babe, everything today is provided by the team. We're going to have a picnic with booths open throughout for beverages."

"Habit." I shrug.

"Come on, you two." He reaches for my hand, and I take it without hesitation. I've missed his touch.

"I need to get her seat," I tell him, stopping next to my SUV and pulling my hand from his.

"I got it covered." He bounces Paisley on his hip as they skip down to his truck, both carefree and laughing. I rush to catch up with them and see a bright pink booster seat in the back of his truck.

"Is this your daughter's?" Paisley asks him.

"No, princess. I bought this for you. I thought it would be nice for you to have a seat in my truck too."

"For me?" she says in awe.

"Just for you," he confirms, setting her in the seat and buckling her in as if he's done it a thousand times. I've lost count of the amount of times this man has brought tears to my eyes for including my daughter, for thinking about her best interests. This one is no exception. I take a deep breath, willing the tears not to fall. He's going to think I'm a blubbering mess, when in reality, these tears are happy. He includes her in everything we do. What more could I ask for in a man?

"You did better," she tells him, referring to the last time he was fumbling to get her buckled.

He laughs. "Can I tell you a secret?" he asks, lowering his voice. She bobs her head up and down. "I practiced. A lot," he adds. "I wanted to make sure you were safe and I was doing it right."

I choke back my tears when she places her little hands on his cheeks and focuses all her attention on him. "You're my best friend," she tells him sweetly.

"And you're my princess." He tweaks her nose before closing the door.

"Thank you," I push the words past my lips.

"I'm just taking care of my girls." He reaches in front of me and opens my door. And it's a good job too as I can barely stop myself from throwing myself at this man. When I'm inside, he places his hand on my thigh and gives it a gentle squeeze. "I've missed you, Ris."

"Me too," I whisper, trying to keep the little ears in the back seat none the wiser of our private confession. He closes my door, and I watch him as he rounds the front of the truck. It's still hard for me to believe this is happening. Can he really be this perfect?

"Who's ready for the zoo?" he asks, pulling out of the lot.

The drive to the zoo is about thirty minutes, and the two of them talk the entire way about all the animals they want to see. They debate which is better—the rhinos or the elephants. Easton never stops smiling, and from the chatter in the back seat, I know Miss P is already having the time of her life garnering all his attention.

By the time we're parked and out of the truck, Paisley is beside herself with excitement. "What are we going to see first?" she asks Easton.

"How about we see it all? We'll start at the beginning and take it all in."

"Yay!" she cheers.

We make our way to the entrance, and Easton gives them his name, retrieving our passes. He places the lanyards around our necks and grabs Paisley's hand. "All right, princess, you ready?" He gets an enthusiastic nod, and then we're off.

He wasn't kidding when he said we would stop at every exhibit. Paisley loves it. The place is deserted compared to the usual crowds, and I'll admit, when an area is overly crowded, I tend to pass it up. With only Blaze members and their families here today, it's a completely different atmosphere.

We're stopped at the gorilla exhibit when Paisley looks up at Easton. "Can I get closer?"

"You can, but no climbing and don't lean on the glass, okay?"

"Okay." She skips off to get a closer look. It's maybe four feet in front of us, but I keep my eyes locked on her.

East steps closer and laces his fingers through mine. "Having fun?" he asks.

"She's loving it."

"I know she is, but I asked about you."

"I am." I don't tell him that it wouldn't matter where we were. If we were with him, we would be having a good time. By the smile on my daughter's face, I can say the same for her.

"You seem tense."

"I'm just... we didn't think about the fact that we would be with your teammates today."

"What does that matter? Hell, we've not even seen many of them, except for in passing."

"You're here with a woman and her kid, Easton. You know they're going to give you shit for that."

"They won't. Not that I would care if they did." He pulls our entwined hands to his lips and kisses my knuckles. "You're more than just some woman, and she's more than just your kid. I want you here, and nothing anyone says will convince me to change my mind. Besides, the guys aren't like that."

Apparently finished with that discussion, he turns to my daughter. "Princess Paisley," he calls out. "You ready for some food? It's almost lunchtime."

"Okay." She skips back toward us and grabs his hand, then reaches for mine. That's how we walk to the event tent that's serving lunch. From the outside looking in, we look like a family, one that I know my little girl craves. Worry starts to ramp up again, but I push it back. He's been nothing but great, and I have to trust in that.

Easton takes charge and grabs two plates, making one for him and one for my daughter. She points out what she wants, and he adds it to her plate. I follow along behind them, watching and listening to their interaction. He sits us at a table with a group of guys who I recognize from that day in the restaurant. "Guys, you remember Larissa," he says with a hint of pride in his voice. "And this is Paisley."

"I'm his princess," she announces, climbing up in the chair he pulled out for her.

"That you are." Easton laughs it off, as if her statement is no big deal.

"I hear you play ball," Fisher says to her.

"Yep. What do you do?" she asks them, just like the little adult she always seems to be.

"We play professional baseball."

"You play with my East?" she asks innocently.

Fisher's eyes flick to Easton, as do mine, and he's staring at my daughter like she lights up his world. "We do," Fisher finally tells her. That seems to be answer enough for her as she picks up her hotdog and takes a big bite.

"Where are your kids?" Paisley asks the group of guys sitting in front of us.

Drew speaks up, "We don't have kids. We're just here to support the team."

She furrows her brow, thinking about what he said. "What about your mommy?"

This causes all the guys to chuckle. "She doesn't live close, but the Blaze, the entire team is our family," he explains.

Her eyes go wide. "That's a big family. I just have my mommy, my grandma, Aunt Chloe, and my East." She ticks off the names on her fingers. Something she started doing a few weeks ago.

"P, you need to eat so we can go see the rest of the animals," I tell her, changing the subject. I'm sure she's giving them way more information than Easton would like.

"Okay, Mommy." She continues to eat, not realizing the heavy conversation she just started. I don't look at the guys or Easton for that matter. I don't want to see the pity in their eyes.

The remainder of lunch breezes by with Paisley stealing the show. Luckily, nothing too heavy after our initial greetings. She rambles on about the exhibits she's seen so far and even convinces the guys that they should play catch with her—of course, she asks Easton if he'll be mad at her if she plays with them. By the time we're finished, my daughter has charmed these big, burly guys. So much so that they all give her a fist bump with the promise of playing catch in the future.

"I think she's had enough," I tell Easton a couple of hours later. Paisley is slowing down, and her excitement wains as exhaustion sets in.

Without a word, he bends down and scoops her up in his arms. She lays her head on his shoulder and snuggles into him, completely trusting. He laces his fingers through mine, and we head toward the exit. Once we reach his truck, he releases my hand and opens the back door to put her in her seat.

"You have fun today, princess?" he asks her.

"Yeah," she says softly. She'll be asleep before we're out of the lot. "East," she calls out for him as he pulls his head out of the truck. Immediately he leans back in.

"What's up?" he asks her.

"I love you," she says, causing my heart to skip a beat.

"Always speak from the heart." His whispered words are husky. It's obvious her words have affected him as well.

"What's that?" her tired voice asks.

"My mom..." He stops. I can imagine him swallowing back his emotions. "My mom used to tell me that all the time when I was little. When you speak from your heart, your true feelings show. She used to tell me you should always be honest with yourself and follow your heart," he tells her.

"Do you— What did you say?" she asks him.

"Speak from your heart."

"Do you speak from your heart?" she asks him.

"I do. Always. I always try to stay true to myself. I don't let what others think convince me to change my mind. I let my heart guide me."

"That's why I love you," she tells him. "And you play with me," she adds, sounding more like the four- going on five-year-old that she is.

There's silence, and then he speaks. His voice is low, so I have to strain to hear him. "I love you too, princess."

I suck in a breath, my heart stilling in my chest. East pulls his head out of the truck and closes the door. His hands land on my hips, and he guides me until my back hits the bed of the truck, out of Paisley's sight. His lips crash to mine. My hands find their way to his hair as I kiss him back with all that I have. There are a million different emotions rushing through me, and I can't decipher which one is more prominent—Worry, fear, gratitude, and, dare I say, love. It's too soon, but damn if my heart doesn't seem to care.

Easton slows the kiss and rests his forehead against mine. "You slay me, both of you. I hope that was okay. I just... she's easy to love."

My heart kick-starts, swelling in my chest. "We should go," I say, because what do I say to that? Tell him that I think if I let myself, I could fall in love with him too? Tell him that if I really sit down and think about it, that I'm already headed down that path? I'm too raw to expose those details just yet. It's too soon. I'm not as open and brave as my daughter. One thing is for sure, if this ends, there are three hearts that will be broken. Of that I'm certain.

CHAPTER 15
Easton

A FTER OUR DAY AT THE ZOO, I flew out the next day for a three-game stretch on the road. We won two of the three. Last night's game was a late one, but this morning's flight is bright and early. Normally I would bitch about the time, but the sooner this plane lifts off, the sooner I can get back to my girls. That's how I think of them now, as my girls. How can I not? They're both becoming necessary, important people in my life.

As soon as we're off the plane, I fire off a text to Larissa.

> We just landed. I'm missing my girls.

Larissa

> Mom is keeping P tonight. I have the early shift at the restaurant tomorrow and the daycare is closed, so Mom took a vacation day.

> I could have watched her.

Larissa:

I couldn't ask you to do that.

> Next time check with me. A day with Princess Paisley sounds like a good time to me.

Larissa:

LOL. You say that now.

> So what time are you taking her to your mom's?

Larissa:

After her game.

> She has a game tonight?

Larissa:

Yes

You're welcome to come.

I read her message and know that inviting me was hard for her. She's cautious when it comes to all things Paisley.

> I'll be home in an hour. I'll send you my address. Come on over. We'll swim and grill out before her game.

You're sure?

Absolutely.

It will be the first time that either of them have been there. I hold my breath, waiting for her reply, wanting them in my space more than I realized.

Larissa:

Okay. Let me get her ball stuff together and a change of clothes.

See you soon, baby.

I'm barely on the road headed home when my phone rings. "Hey, Dad," I answer after seeing his name come across the dash.

"East, how are you, son?"

"Good, just leaving the airport."

"That's why I'm calling. You had three damn good games."

"Did Mark tell you that?" I tease. It's a running joke in our family that Uncle Mark loves the game more than Dad. He could have gone pro but had a knee injury that kept him in the dugout.

"Very funny, smartass." He laughs good-naturedly. "So, what's up? Your mom mentioned she hasn't talked to you much lately."

I don't even hesitate to tell him. "I met someone."

"Tell me more." I can imagine him sitting back in his chair, propping his legs up on his desk.

"She's gorgeous and sweet, and she has a little girl. She's four."

"Have you met her?"

"Yeah, we've hung out a few times. Great kid."

"Not that you need the reminder, but as your father, that's my job. There are three hearts at stake here, Easton."

"I know that, Dad. Trust me, I do. I also know that my heart... it races anytime she's near," I confess.

"This sounds all too familiar to me," he says with a laugh.

"When did you know?" I ask him. "When did it hit you that Mom and I were what you wanted?"

"I knew the night I met her. I hadn't met you yet, but you're an extension of her, and I never stood a chance not to love either one of you."

"I'm in deep, Dad."

"Of course you are. You're a Monroe. That's how we do it, all-in. When do we get to meet them? And you need to call your mother," he chastises.

I laugh. "Soon, I hope. I'll call Mom, I promise."

"Good. Take care, son."

"You too and, Dad..." I pause, giving my words the attention they need. "I love you."

"Love you too, son." I can hear the emotion in his voice before the line goes dead. Jeff Monroe is the type of man I want to be. He loves us unconditionally, and that's what I want to do for my girls. I want to take the worry from Larissa's eyes and replace it with the carefree happiness I've only seen a glimpse of. I want to be at Paisley's games and scare the shit out of her dates when they come to pick her up when she's thirty. I can see our future, picture it in my mind. I just need Ris to catch up.

When I pull into the driveway, her SUV is already there. I hit the button on the garage door and pull in, opening the second door as well. When I climb out of my truck, I motion for her to pull in.

"Why?" she asks, rolling down her window.

"Just humor me."

She rolls those big green eyes and shakes her head, but she pulls into the second bay. I head to the back to help Paisley out of her seat, but she beats me to it. "I didn't think you would ever get here," she says in a sassy yet cute way only she can pull off.

"I know. I was gone forever," I agree with her. I, too, feel as though it took me forever to get them here. To be home with them.

"Your house is really big," Paisley says, latching onto my hand.

"You think so?" I ask her, and she nods.

Larissa climbs out, and without thinking, I snake my free hand around her waist and pull her into me, placing a quick kiss to her lips. "I missed you," I whisper.

"What about me?" Paisley asks. "Did you miss me? I didn't get a kiss," she points out.

Bending, I pick her up in my arms, settle her on my hip, and kiss her on the cheek. "I missed both of you." I tickle her sides, causing her to laugh. "Come on, ladies, the pool is calling our name."

"I gots a game tonight, so I can't get too tired, right, Mommy?" Paisley asks.

"That's right, sweetie. I say we swim and then maybe catch a nap?"

"I don't like naps," Paisley grumbles.

"Really?" I ask her, a schooled expression on my face. "I love naps. I would nap every single day if I could."

"You do?" Her eyes are wide.

"Sure. Everyone loves naps."

"Will you take one with me?" she asks.

"Of course I will. We can all take a nap after our swim. How does that sound?"

"Really good," she agrees. I smile over at Larissa, and she just shakes her head.

About an hour of splashing around in the pool, and I can tell Princess Paisley is wearing down. "I'm tired," I say, faking a yawn, covering my mouth.

"Yeah, me too," she says, mimicking me.

"What do you say we take that nap?"

"Yeah, Mommy, you ready for a nap?" she asks Larissa.

"I think so." Larissa stretches in her barely-there bikini. It's really uncomfortable to be sporting wood and playing in the pool with a four-year-old. I had to keep my distance from her mother. That's all I need to do is traumatize Paisley for life. Her mother on the other hand....

"Y'all can change in my room. I'll grab some clothes and change across the hall." I rush up the stairs and grab some basketball shorts, underwear, and a T-shirt out of my dresser. "I'll be done in a minute." I change quickly, leaving my wet clothes hanging on the side of the tub.

When I knock on my bedroom door, Paisley announces for me to come in. They're sitting on the edge of the bed while Larissa braids her hair. "You ready for that nap?" I ask her.

"Where are we sleeping?"

"Here," I tell her, finding Larissa's eyes. Heat flares between us.

"Is this your room?" Paisley asks.

"Yeah, you think my bed is big enough for all three of us?"

"Yes. It's the most biggest bed I've ever seen. Mommy said I'm not allowed to jump on it."

"Did she?"

"Yeah," she says, dejected.

"What if I told you that when you wake up from your nap, you can jump on my bed?"

"I say it's time for a nap." She crawls from the foot of the bed to the top and pulls back my dark gray comforter. "This is gray like my name," she informs us.

"Wow, you're super smart," I tell her with a smile.

"I know," she replies, climbing under the covers, making me laugh and Larissa scold her about her manners.

I move to stand behind Larissa. "Ready for your nap, baby?" I ask, trailing my index finger down her back.

"Y-yes," she sputters before climbing in and curling up beside Paisley. I take a minute to commit the scene before me to memory. If I have my say, there will be many, many more days just like this one, but in the event it doesn't turn out that way, I never want to forget this moment.

"East, you're 'posta be napping," Paisley reminds me.

"Let me get the light." I turn off the light and then walk to the windows and pull the blinds, blocking out the sun. When I climb into bed, Paisley grabs my hand and pulls me closer to them. She then grabs Larissa hand and places it in mine, settling our joined hands on her lap and resting hers on top of ours. "Night, night, family," she says, closing her eyes.

My eyes find Larissa's, and I see her tears brimming. I want to pull her into my arms and kiss her soft lips. I want to tell her that I want to take naps like this every day. I want to tell her that I want to be their family. Instead, I give her hand a gentle squeeze. She closes her eyes and snuggles up to Paisley. We lie there in the quiet room, nothing but the sound of our even breathing. When her hand goes lax in mine, I know she's asleep. When Paisley rolls over and snuggles up into her mom's chest, I feel a pang of longing in mine. Careful not to wake them, I slide over and wrap my arms around both of them. Once I have them where they are meant to be, I'm able to fall asleep.

CHAPTER 16
Larissa

I WAS A LITTLE WORRIED about East being at Paisley's game, but it worked out. The dads were eager to meet him, and the moms were eager to talk to him. All the while, he stood there with his hand in mine or his arm over my shoulders, and after they won the game, my daughter was in his arms. When a guy from the other team asked him for his autograph, he asked him to call the main office and he would get it to him, but today he was with his family.

"I like being your family, East," Paisley says before biting into her hot dog that he just grilled for her. We're sitting on his back deck having dinner. Hot dogs and hamburgers on the grill.

"You do?"

"Yep."

"Well, I like it too," he tells her.

"Can I stay here instead of going to Grandma's?" she asks.

"No, sweetie. Mommy has to be at work early tomorrow," I answer.

"I can stay with East." She says this like we should have already figured out that was the best answer.

"Sorry, princess. We have to listen to what Mommy says. I fly out on Tuesday, but I'll be back Thursday afternoon. Maybe we can have dinner here?"

"Where you going?"

"I have a game in Chicago. Then I have two games here at home, one Friday and one Sunday. Maybe you and your mom can come and watch me play?"

"Can we, Mommy?"

He looks over at me, waiting for my answer. "We'll see if we can get tickets to the game on Sunday."

"Babe, you don't need to get tickets. I have that covered. You just need to tell me if you want to sit with the other wives and girlfriends or in the stands behind the dugout."

"Which one is closer to you?" Paisley asks. She has no idea that my heart is beating like a bass drum in my chest at him referring to me as his girlfriend.

"The dugout."

"I wanna sit by you," she tells him.

"Ris?"

"Dugout it is. You sure it's okay?" I ask, chewing on my bottom lip.

"Positive," he replies, grinning wildly.

"What's the big grin for?" I ask. It's causing a flurry of butterflies in my belly. Easton Monroe is gorgeous, but when he pulls out the big guns and you're on the receiving end of one of his megawatt smiles, he's breathtaking. That's the only word I can think of to describe him.

"My girls are coming to watch me play," he says simply.

We finish dinner, and I pack up Paisley's things to take her to Mom's. "Thank you for today," I tell him.

"You're coming back, right?"

"Uh, I.... Do you want me to?"

"Ris," he says, snaking an arm around my waist.

I look into the kitchen where Paisley is sitting at the table playing on her tablet. "I wasn't sure," I confess.

"I want you here as much as possible. I like the two of you being here."

"Okay. I need to go home and change, but I can come back."

"Pack whatever you need to spend the night."

"Okay." I repeat the answer, because really, I don't know what else to say. I want to spend more time with him. I want more of his touches, more of his kisses. I'm too far gone to turn back now. If things were to end today, Paisley and I would both have broken hearts. Might as well forge ahead. I can hear Chloe's voice in my head telling me to take chances.

"Be safe," he says, kissing me quickly.

"I'll be back soon."

"I'll be here." He kisses me yet again and then pulls away. He walks to where Paisley is sitting at the table and lifts her into his arms. "You be good for Grandma, okay?"

"I will." She hugs him as tight as her little arms will allow.

Easton walks us to my SUV that's parked in his garage. He buckles Paisley into her seat, kisses her cheek and shuts the door. "Drive safe, Ris." He kisses my forehead then opens my door for me. "Wait." He jogs over to a shelf on the wall and brings back a small plastic remote. "Here's a garage door opener. Just come on in when you get back." Reaching in, he clips it to my visor. He waits until I'm buckled in before closing the door and standing back, watching us drive away.

When we get to Mom's, Paisley has to tell her all about our day with Easton. Mom smiles and asks questions, all while wearing a knowing grin. When Paisley runs into the house, Mom asks me when she gets to meet him. Honestly, I thought about inviting him to come with me, but I needed a minute to breathe, to process this freight train we seem to be riding. Things are moving fast, and normally, I would be scared out of my mind. The worry is there, but Easton, he just makes it easy. I've never had that, not even with Steve. There's something about him that calms me. Maybe it's the way he's so open with how he feels, about how he wants to see where this takes us. Maybe it's because he told my daughter he loves her. Either way, it's a lot to process.

I promise Mom it will be soon, kiss Paisley goodbye, and hightail it out of there, making it to my place in record time. I grab the clothes I'll need for work tomorrow, my toiletries, and some clothes to sleep in, just in case. I'm now sitting on the end of the bed, debating if going back is the right decision. I know he's waiting for me; I also know that the chemistry between us is undeniable. I've only slept with one man in my life, and if I go back there, that's going to change. I know that, and so does he. The question is, am I ready for that? My body's ready and has been for a while. His hands are like magic, his kisses like candy. But my heart and my head, are they ready?

I think about how good he is to me, how he's been upfront and all-in from the night we met. I think about how great he is with Paisley, and I know I have my answer. I loved my husband, but I'm still young, and I miss having a man's arms wrapped around me. I miss the touches, the sex. I miss all of it.

Decision made, I double-check I have everything I need, lock up my apartment, and head back to his place. As soon as I make the turn to pull into his driveway, the garage door opens and Easton's standing there, as if he's been there waiting since I pulled out. I park and climb out of the car, only to be pushed up against the passenger door of his truck and have his lips welded to mine.

"I missed you," he says against my lips.

"I was gone maybe an hour," I say with a laugh. I don't mention that he didn't give me the opportunity to use the garage door opener.

"That's too long, Ris. Too fucking long." His lips trail across my jaw and down my neck. I tilt my head, giving him better access. "I need to get you inside." He nips at my earlobe and steps away, grabbing my hand and leading me inside. He hits the button of the garage door on the way in. I watch as we stop at a small white box on the wall and he engages the alarm system, then let him guide me upstairs to his room.

In his room, he turns to face me. I expect him to kiss me again, but he doesn't. Instead, he pulls his T-shirt over his head and drops it to the floor. All the while, his eyes are locked on mine. Before I arrived, I'd already decided I was all-in for wherever this ride leads us, so I follow suit. I lift my tank top up and over my head, dropping it on top of his shirt. There's a slight tremble in my hands. It's been a long time for me.

Eyes still locked with mine, he pushes his shorts to the floor, stepping out of them. Tit for tat, I unzip my jeans shorts and slide them down my legs, kicking them to the side as well.

"I can't believe you're here." His voice is a husky whisper. "I've thought about this moment so many times."

Feeling brave from the hunger in his eyes, I reach behind my back and unclasp my bra. Slowly, I drop one strap then the other, holding the cups in place. His eyes burn with intensity, the brown orbs looking black from desire. I drop my bra at my feet, leaving us both in nothing but boxer briefs and a thin black lace thong.

CHAPTER 17
Easton

I JUST ABOUT SWALLOW MY fucking tongue. The woman before me is perfect. The swell of her breasts and her pert pink nipples beg for my mouth. I thought I'd know what I was going to see from her barely there bikini but that scrap of thread was hiding more than I could have imagined.

All of her.

Every inch is perfection.

Stepping forward, I test the weight of her breast in the palm of my hand. Firm. Round. Perfect. Not able to hold back, I bend my head and suck one into my mouth, nipping her tight nipple with my teeth, then soothing it with my tongue.

"East," she murmurs, which only fuels my desire. Moving my mouth to her other breast, I lavish it with attention as well. Before the night is through, I want my tongue to have traced every inch of her.

"What, baby?" I ask. I know damn well what she wants.

Me.

She's in luck, because I want her just as fiercely. Stepping back from her, I make quick work of stripping out of my boxer briefs. "I need you naked, Ris." She doesn't hesitate to pull the thin scrap of fabric down her legs. "On the bed, baby." Again, she complies and climbs up on the bed, where just hours ago we slept with her daughter between us.

A family.

Paisley's words ring in my ears. I want that. I want them. I won't stop until I prove that to her. On my knees, I settle between her legs, taking my fill of her. "You're mine now, Larissa. I can't come back from this moment. Tell me you understand that." This need I have for her, for them to be in my life is strong. I know it's fast, but damn if I want it to slow down. Not until I know they're mine.

She nods.

"I need your words, baby." Reaching out, I trace the lips of her pussy with my index finger, causing her to whimper.

"I'm yours," she pants.

"Both of you, Ris. Not just you. I need both my girls." I don't know why, but it feels important that I clarify that before I make love to her. She nods again, which is good enough for me. Reaching into the nightstand, I grab a condom and roll it down my hard length. "I want to drive you wild. I want to kiss every inch of your skin, but right now, I need you. I promise I'll make it up to you, but right now...." I don't know how to tell her of this need I have inside me without sounding like a selfish prick.

Turns out I don't have to. Larissa reaches between us and palms me, stroking root to tip. She then aligns me with her entrance, lifting her hips, showing me she wants me just as badly as I want her. Leaning over her, I brace my weight on my arms on either side of her head.

"I've only been with Paisley's dad," she whispers.

The reality of what that means, that after all these years, I'm the man she's letting into her world, into her body, is humbling.

Slowly, I slide inside her, inch by inch, giving her body time to adjust. When I'm fully seated, I bury my face in her neck and focus on breathing. She's so fucking tight. I've never felt anything quite like it. Electricity pulses through my veins, my breathing labored, and my heart feels as though it could barrel right out of my chest. All I've done is slide inside her. I'm still, she's still, and it's the most profound moment of my life.

Lifting my head, I look down at her. Holding my weight on one hand, I use the other to push her hair out of her face. "I'm the last," I tell her. Her hands are under my arms, gripping my back, her legs locked tight around my ass. Confusion mars her beautiful face. I need to move. My cock is pulsing inside her, begging me to move. I need to make sure she understands before I do. "He was your first, Ris, and I'm your last."

A tear slides down her cheek. I drop my head and kiss it away then begin to move. Pulling my hips back, I slowly slide home again. That's what she feels like—home. I've barely been inside her, and that fact is obvious. There will never be anyone like her.

She's the one.

Her hips lift as I quicken my strokes, powering in and out of her. I'm a man on a mission. "You feel so good," I manage to say, thrusting in and out of her over and over again.

"There," she says when I roll my hips. "That," she instructs.

I do it again, and her muscles tighten around my cock. "I need you there, Ris. I'm so fucking close," I warn her.

"T-there," she moans deep in the back of her throat. Her pussy is going crazy as it squeezes the fuck out of my cock.

"That's it, baby." I swivel my hips again, just how she likes it. Her nails dig into my back, and her legs are locked around me like a vise. Her head tilts back, and she cries out my name. She's squeezing my cock, milking me as I release inside her, following her over the edge of the bliss we've created together.

Sliding out of her, I fall beside her on the bed, pulling her into my arms, where she's practically lying on top of me. I kiss the top of her head, holding on to her like my life depends on it. "You wreck me," I pant.

"Is it always like this? I don't remember sex being so... explosive."

"That's us, baby. It's never felt like that before. Never," I assure her.

"How long until we can do that again?"

"I need a little time. Let me catch my breath."

Her hands trail up and down my abs. "You said some stuff," she says cautiously.

"Uh-huh." I'm still having trouble breathing regularly. I wasn't kidding when I told her she wrecked me.

"Was it the moment? I won't hold it against you if it was, but I just... need to know."

"Fuck that." My words come out a little more forcefully than I intended them to. "I meant every word. You're mine now. No man will ever feel your wrecking powers," I say, making her chuckle.

"Maybe," she says, a playful tone to her voice. "I reserve the right to amend my agreement after round two."

"I'll show you round two." I stand from the bed to dispose of the condom, grabbing another from the drawer on my way back through. I proceed to prove to her over and over again all through the night, that her decision to stay with me was the right one.

CHAPTER 18
Larissa

WAKING UP IN HIS ARMS is something I could get used to. My back is to his chest, and I can feel his hot breath against my neck. It's comforting, and I never want to leave. I want to stay in this bed, with his strong arms wrapped around me. I want to live in this fantasy world we've created. Last night, he made a lot of declarations, ones he swears are true, but I'm not so naïve to know that things change in the light of day. I know that words are exchanged in the heat of the moment, and when that moment fizzles, when the intensity and the high are gone, regret takes its place. Me, I have no regrets. I meant every word, every touch, but Easton... well, he might not have. That's why I'm lying here in his arms, still, afraid to move an inch, not wanting this fantasy to be over.

His lips press against my bare shoulder. "Morning, beautiful." His husky voice washes over me. "How did you sleep?"

"Did we sleep?" I ask, teasing him. I lost count of the number of times we reached for each other in the night.

"We did. We did more than that," he says, cupping my naked breast. "We should make this a nightly thing," he suggests.

"You have practice in an hour. You'll regret those words I'm sure by the time you're done."

"Never," he says, pulling my body closer to his. "I could never regret anything when it comes to you."

"Morning changes things." I put it out there—the worry he'll change his mind.

"You're right. It does," he agrees. I stiffen in his arms. I thought I was prepared for this, but I was wrong. "You're even more beautiful today than you were yesterday," he says, once again pressing his lips to my bare shoulder.

I release an audible breath and relax into his hold.

"I can't explain it, Ris, but fuck, I don't even want to. I don't care that this is fast. I don't care if someone thinks it too soon. It feels right. You feel right. That's all that matters to me. You and P are... everything. That's the best way I can describe it. I want you, both of you. I meant every word I said last night. No man..." He runs his hand over my belly, until he reaches my center. "...will ever be here." He traces his fingers through my folds. "You're mine now."

"Does that work both ways?"

"Hell yes, it does. I don't want anyone but you. You're all I see, all I think about."

"I have baggage," I remind him. I hate referring to my daughter as baggage, but my life is not my own.

"You have a beautiful little girl who has stolen my heart."

Turning over in his arms, I run my hand over the stubble that covers his cheeks. "Are you real?" I ask him.

He chuckles. "Yeah, babe, I'm real."

"I just... the things you say, it's—"

"From my heart."

Tears prick my eyes as I remember his conversation with Paisley about always speaking from your heart. "Yeah?"

He leans in and kisses me softly. "Always, Larissa."

"You need to get ready for practice, and I have to get ready for work."

"I don't want to move."

"You have to." I poke him in the side, causing him to squirm.

"You have plans tonight?"

"Nope, just picking P up from Mom's after my shift."

"Will you come back here? I can make us dinner. P can swim."

"We can do that," I say, kissing his chin.

"Pack a bag for both of you."

"I don't think that's such a good idea."

He pulls away so he can see me. "What? Why not?"

"I don't want Paisley to get the wrong idea. She's already attached to you. I don't need her to see us sleeping in the same bed."

"She's already seen it," he counters.

"That was a nap in the middle of the day. Not at night."

"I want you here, both of you."

"We'll come for a visit, but we're going back to our place."

"For now," he concedes. "You'll see this isn't a game to me. I get that it's more than just you and me that is going to be affected by our actions, by the decisions that we make. I lived that. I've been on your side of the fence. I'm not going into this lightly."

"I know that." Reaching up, I run my fingers through his hair. "I know, but I just need some time. Okay. I'm yours," I rush to tell him. "I meant what I said last night, but I need some time to get used to the idea. To warm Paisley up to the idea."

"She loves me." He grins, looking cocksure and adorable.

"I know she does. I just don't want her heart to be broken if this doesn't work out."

"Oh, it's going to work out." He lowers his mouth to mine, tracing my lips with his tongue. "It's going to more than work out." He kisses me, deep and slow. His lips soft yet firm against my own. "I'll give you some time to catch up to where I am. I want you." He kisses my nose. "I want Paisley." He kisses my forehead. "I want us." He kisses my lips. Just a soft peck, but the emotion behind it, the words before it makes it seem so much more.

"Shower," I mumble against his lips. "I won't be the reason you're in hot water for being late to practice."

"You're worth it," he says, kissing down my column of my neck.

"I can't be late for work."

"Fine," he grumbles good-naturedly. He climbs out of bed and before I realize what's going on, he has me thrown over his shoulder and stalking toward the bathroom.

"Wh-what are you doing?" I ask, laughing.

"We're taking a shower."

"We both know we'll be late if we take a shower together."

"I promise to be on my best behavior." He sets me on the counter. "I just want you with me." He shrugs casually, as if his words don't take my breath away.

I watch him as he starts the shower, tests the temperature of the water, then turns and holds his hand out for me. I take it, hopping off the counter and stepping in behind him. His shower is huge, so much so it makes me think of that Nickelback song where they talk about a bathroom you can play baseball in, and laugh.

"What's so funny?"

"Nothing, this is huge."

He looks down at his cock, which is saluting me and grins. "I know."

I roll my eyes but can't keep the smile off my face. I know all too well how "huge" he is. I can still feel him. "I meant the shower," I say, reaching for his shampoo.

"I want to do that." He takes a step toward me.

"Stop!" I hold out my hand to stop his movement. "You can't help me. We'll never get out of here, and I can't be late for work."

He juts his lip out and bats those big brown eyes at me. "Let me," he whispers.

"Best behavior, mister. I am not going to be late for work."

He grumbles something under his breath, but steps back under the spray, on his side of the shower. I think this is the first time I've ever showered wearing what feels like a permanent grin. Easton makes life fun. He makes me want to wake up like this, make this showering together our daily routine. I can't help but send up a silent prayer that one day it will be.

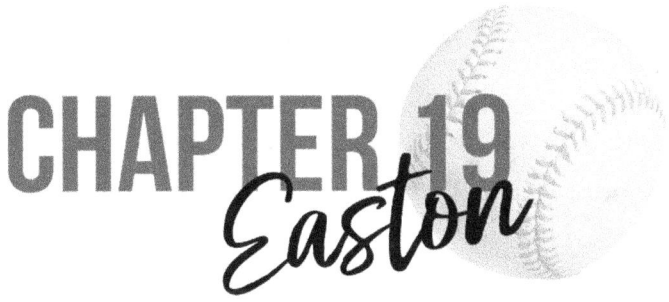

CHAPTER 19
Easton

I STEP BACK UNDER THE spray and away from her. I know this job is her livelihood. I almost told her to quit and let me take care of them, but I know better than to do that. I want her to reach her dreams, her goals in life. I know working at The Vineyard is not hers, but it's what puts food on the table for her and Paisley. So instead, I give in and let the hot water pour over me as I keep my eyes glued to her. Her eyes are closed as she lathers her hair and tilts her head back to rinse away the shampoo. Water and soap slides down over her breasts, and I want nothing more than to touch her there, everywhere. She's my addiction.

"Do you have conditioner?" she asks.

"No," I choke out the word. I'm so consumed with lust for her that speaking when she's naked, wet, and just a few feet away is almost impossible.

"Okay." She grabs my bodywash, pours some in the palm of her hand, rubs them together and then lathers them all over her body.

I ball my hands into fists at my sides, fighting the urge to take over. My cock is hard as steel as I watch her. I'm half tempted to take care of it here and now. I imagine her wet body sliding against mine as she grips my cock, root to tip, slowly driving me mad. If it were not for the fact that I know that the real thing, her heat, is better than any self-induced orgasm I could bring for myself, I would. There is also the small factor of both of us being late. I can see the hunger in her eyes, though; it's not just me who's turned on, but I respect her and the fact she refuses to be late to work. Besides, this thing between us is a marathon, not a sprint.

"You good, Monroe?" she asks me. Her smile is infectious.

"You done?"

She throws her head back and laughs. "Yeah, I'm done." She saunters out of the shower.

I have to close my eyes to keep from following her. My cock is steel, so I reach for the nozzle and turn the water to cold. I cringe as it hits my heated skin, but desperate times call for desperate measures. I don't need to be rolling up into practice with a bat between my legs. I'm all for kidding around, but the guys would never let me live that one down. Once I've got things under control, I rush through the rest of my shower in the ice-cold water, not taking any chances.

I take my time drying off, hoping Larissa has had time to get dressed. Giving her time to cover her gorgeous body, not that it makes a difference. Clothed or naked I crave her.

"How long's practice?" she asks when I enter the bedroom. She's fully clothed in her black pants and black button-down, her uniform for The Vineyard.

"All day. We hit the weights, then the field, then watch film."

"Wow. All day. I just assumed a few hours or something."

"I mean, yeah, I'm that good. The others, they need all the help they can get." I smirk.

"Uh-huh," she responds with a laugh. "I think the next time I see Drew, I'll get his opinion on the matter," she teases.

I stalk toward her and lift her in my arms, her feet dangling from the floor. "You trying to make me jealous?"

"No, but are you?"

"You're damn right I am." I press my lips to hers quickly, then set her back on her feet. "I can't get caught up in you right now," I confess. "Any longer and neither one of us will be leaving this room today."

She smiles up at me. Her eyes are sparkling, and my chest swells knowing I put that sparkle there. It's as if she's finally opening up to me, and even though I never thought it would be possible, she's even more beautiful. Maybe it's because I know she's mine.

"So, you sure you want us to come back here tonight, you don't want a break?"

"I leave tomorrow and won't be back until Thursday."

"I know, I understand if you want a break before you leave."

I snake an arm around her waist and pull her close. "The only thing I want are my girls here with me, so I can soak up as much of the two of you as I can before I go on the road."

"Yeah?" I can hear the hope in her voice.

"Yes. Pick up Princess P and get your asses here as soon as you can. I'll grab dinner on my way home."

"I thought we would just throw something on the grill?"

"I'm thinking P would like some cheese pizza more."

"You can't be spoiling her," she says with a stern voice. One that doesn't faze me.

"Sure I can. She's my princess." I kiss her nose and release her from my hold. "I gotta go. I'll see you tonight." A quick kiss to her lips and I'm walking away from her toward the bedroom door.

"Wait!" she calls out. "I'm almost done. I'll come with you." She rushes to grab her clothes and stuff them back in her bag.

"It's fine. You have some time yet. I'll check the patio and front doors. Just make sure you shut the garage door with the opener I gave you and it's all good." I stalk back to her, because I can, and kiss her one more time. "Have a good day, Ris." With that, I hustle out of the room, grab my keys and wallet, and rush out the door.

Twenty minutes later, I'm walking into the locker room still wearing a shit-eating grin.

"What's got you looking like you just hit a grand slam in the bottom of the ninth?" Drew asks, taking a seat on the bench next to me.

"What? Can a guy not have a good day?"

"Sure he can, but that"—he points to the grin I can't seem to control—"is more than just a good day."

I nod. "Life is good, my man. Just living the dream."

He studies me, and a slow grin tilts his lips. "Larissa."

"A gentleman never tells," I chide, placing my phone, keys, and wallet in my locker.

"Since when?" he asks, crossing his arms over his chest.

"Since Larissa," I confess.

"No shit." He smacks his hand on my shoulder. "You finally wore her down?"

"Finally," I agree. For a while there, I wasn't sure she was ever going to give me a chance.

"You ready for all that? She's a mom, East."

"I'm ready," I assure him. I have zero fears about the fact that Larissa is a single mom. Hell, if anything, it endears her to me even more. I know what single moms go through, the fight to make ends meet, the struggle to be both parents. She's one of the strongest women I know.

He nods, and that ends our conversation. He knows me. I'm a man of my word. If I'm in, I'm in, and when it comes to Larissa and Paisley, there is no other way to be.

CHAPTER 20
Larissa

TODAY SEEMS AS IF IT'S dragging by. I know it's because of the anticipation of seeing Easton again. It's scary and exciting.

I still worry about Paisley getting too attached, but I can't protect her from life. I wish that I could, but I know the reality is if I do that, she'll never be prepared to be on her own one day. One day, far, far away that I don't want to think about.

"Hey," Chloe greets me. "You been here all day?"

"Yeah, I had the early shift. I have an hour to go," I say, looking at my watch.

"Rough day?" She laughs.

"Actually, no we've been steady. I'm just ready to go."

"Uh-huh. And why is that? You got a hot date?"

"I'm picking P up at Mom's right after work."

"You're avoiding my question."

"It's not a date."

"Riigghhttt." She drags out the word. "Sure it's not."

"Catch me up on what's been going on in your life."

I look up at the screen hoping to see my section full so we don't have to talk about this. Not that I don't talk to Chloe, I do. She's been there for me through so much, but this relationship with Easton is new, and I'm afraid to talk about it. I don't want to jinx it. That's the worrier in me.

"Living the dream, how about you?" she turns it back on me.

"Nothing to report," I lie.

She gives me the "I know you're full of shit" look and crosses her arms over her chest. "Try again."

"Fine, we've been hanging out. He calls and texts a lot. He went to P's game yesterday."

"Did he now?" She smirks. "I'm guessing he was the main attraction?"

"The parents, both moms and dads, were falling all over themselves to meet him, to talk to him. The kids were awestruck...." I trail off thinking about it.

"What are you not telling me?"

"Nothing, he was great. When he was asked for an autograph, he told them he was with his family and to call the main office and he would get it for them, but not then."

"So now you're his family?" Her smile is so big I think I can actually hear it, the happiness in the sound of her voice.

"It was just a way for him to get out of signing autographs. We would have been there all night."

She studies me a few minutes, and I try not to squirm under her gaze. "What else?"

"Nothing, we hung out at his place beforehand."

"Damn, Larissa, it's like pulling teeth to get any information out of you. What gives?"

"I just... I don't want to jinx it. I really like him, and Paisley, I think she's already getting attached to him too. It's all happening so fast."

"You're the only one who can judge how fast or slow whatever it is you two have goes. If it feels right, it feels right. P is a strong little girl. She can handle it. You can't shelter her from getting hurt her entire life."

"I know that. I do, and I'm letting him in. It just seems like it's been a whirlwind. He calls us 'his girls'." I try to hide my smile, but it's pointless.

"Spill." She narrows her eyes at me as she laughs.

"Fine, we went to his place and swam, then took a nap, went to P's game, then I took P to Mom's, went back to his place and stayed the night."

"Who took a nap?" she asks.

"We all did."

"Where?"

"His bed."

"Larissa!" she says, exasperated.

"The three of us lay down on his monster of a bed. Paisley between us and took a nap with her before her game."

"Aww." She smiles.

"Then after her game, we ate, and I took P to Mom's. He asked me to pack a bag and come back, so I did. I stayed there last night."

"And?" she prompts.

"And it was nice."

"Nice? Nice is for a neighbor dropping off some cookies at the holidays. Nice is not for spending the night with the first baseman for the Tennessee Blaze. Look, I get it. It's personal and I know it's the first time since Steve, but just tell me this. Did he take care of you?"

My face flames. It's been so long for me that talking about sex, outside of joking about not getting any, is uncommon. "It was amazing. *He's* amazing."

"That's my girl." She holds up her hand to give me a high-five. I contemplate leaving her hanging but decide against it and slap my hand against hers. "So, when are you seeing him again?"

"Tonight," I say, feeling my face turn hot. "He asked me to come over as soon as I get off. I'm picking P up and we're going to his place for dinner."

"Don't forget to pack a bag." She grins.

"Yeah, he wanted me to. I told him no. I think it's a little too early for sleepovers. Paisley is already enamored with him."

"Your pace, Larissa." She looks at her watch.

I nod, looking at my watch. Finally, it's time to go home. "I'll see you later," I say, already walking toward the computer hanging on the wall to clock out.

Paisley comes running out of the house as soon as I pull into the driveway. "Mommy!"

"Hey, girlie," I pick her up and swing her around. She's growing up so fast I won't be able to do this much longer. "How was your day?"

"So so fun. Gram and I went to the park!" she says excitedly.

"That does sound fun."

"Hey, sweetheart, how was work?" Mom asks.

"Good. It was a long day. Thanks for watching her."

"You know I wouldn't have it any other way," she tells me. "She was an angel, as always."

I smile down at Paisley, and I'm just about to comment on her being good when Mom adds, "She seems rather fond of Easton."

"He's a nice guy." I don't tell her that Paisley isn't the only one who's fond of him.

"From the stories I've heard, it seems as if he is. When do I get to meet him?"

"Mom, we're just... friends, I guess? Getting to know each other. We're not there yet." I can't help but think about him calling me his girlfriend. Mom would have a field day if she knew that. I smile to myself. I like having that moment be ours. I want to keep every memory with him to myself. It's as if I were to share it with the world, he'll disappear. Maybe this has all been a dream? It sure feels like one. Easton is most definitely a dream come true. He's everything I could want in a partner, boyfriend, whatever it is I'm supposed to call him.

"He's good with her?" she questions.

My eyes prick with tears, because he is. He's incredible with my daughter. "Yeah, he's good with her. Too good, in fact. I fear if this... whatever it is turns into something, he's going to spoil her rotten."

"Nothing wrong with that."

"Mommy, what are we having for dinner? My belly's talking to me."

"It is? What's it saying?"

"That it wants pizza."

We don't eat out a lot. One, it gets expensive and two, I like to make sure she's getting a balanced diet. I want to tell her that Easton is getting pizza, but I decide to surprise her instead. Let him be the one who tells her. It was his idea after all. I can't help but let my mind wander to the last four years. Is this what it would have been like? Sharing the parenting responsibilities? My mom is wonderful and has helped me so much, but it's different.

"We'll have to see. Go grab your bag so we can go. Gram needs a break."

"I's got it on the porch." She takes off running back to the porch, grabs her bag, and is back in no time.

"To have her energy," Mom muses.

"Right?" I laugh. "Thanks again, Mom. I have the evening shift the next two days."

"I'll be ready and waiting for her."

Leaning in, I wrap my arms around her and hug her tightly. There's no way I could have done this on my own. My mom has been here every step of the way and given me more than she will ever know. One day, I hope to be in a job where she does not have to watch Paisley in the evenings. Where she can just be Gram and have sleepovers and play dates, and not the babysitter.

One day.

CHAPTER 21
Easton

W HEN I PULL INTO THE driveway, I see the garage door lifting and Larissa pulling in. We could not have timed this better if we tried. Practice was long and grueling. Afterward, I stopped by and picked up dinner. I got Paisley her own cheese pizza, me a meat lovers, and another large cheese. I'll eat anything, but I'm not sure what Larissa likes on her pizza. The other night when we went out, we just ordered cheese for the table.

Hitting the button on my visor, the other garage door opens just as Larissa is climbing out of her SUV. By the time I'm pulled in and grab the pizzas from the back seat, Paisley is wrapping her little arms around my legs.

"East! I'm so, so happy to see you. And you gots pizza." She speaks with such joy, I can't help but smile at her.

"I did. I thought you might be in the mood for some cheesy pie." I brush some of her loose curls out of her eyes.

"Pie? Pizza isn't pie, silly." She finishes with a laugh.

"But it's shaped like one. It's a pizza pie."

This time I'm greeted with a soft giggle. "Pizza pie," she sings.

"All right, Miss P, let him go so we can head inside and eat." Larissa reaches for her hand and Paisley takes it.

Pizza in one arm, I snake the other out and around her waist, guiding her into my arms. I place a kiss on her temple. "Missed you," I whisper.

"What about me, did you miss me too, East?" Paisley asks in her sweet voice. It almost sounds as if she's worried my answer might be no. As if it ever could be no when it comes to her.

I hand Larissa the pizza, then bend down and lift Paisley in my arms, settling her on my hip. "Of course I missed you. I missed both my girls."

Her eyes widen. "We're your girls?"

"Yep." I kiss her on the temple, just as I did her mother seconds before. "You hungry?"

"So, so hungry. My belly was talking to me."

"No way." I feign disbelief.

Her little head bobs up and down. "Uh-huh, and it was telling me it wanted pizza. Ask Mommy."

"Mommy?" I turn to face Larissa. "Did you hear this conversation?"

Larissa's eyes sparkle with what I hope is amusement and happiness. "No, but Miss P informed me that her belly indeed did ask for pizza. You must be a belly reader."

"A belly reader?" Paisley asks.

"Yeah, he knows what your belly wants when it's hungry."

"Do you hear pizza?" Paisley asks innocently.

"I sure do. I even heard that you wanted your very own pizza." Her eyes widen. "Let's get you inside so we can eat." With Paisley on my hip, I follow Larissa into the house, hitting the buttons to close the garage doors on the way.

"Where do you want to sit?" Larissa asks.

I look down at Paisley who is still in my arms. "What do you think, princess? Should we eat inside or out on the deck?"

"It's really hot out there," she says, her face stone serious.

"Inside it is." I chuckle. Carrying her inside, I stop at the island and sit her in one of the chairs. "Don't wiggle around too much. I don't want you to fall."

"East," she says, exasperated. "I'm four. I'll be five.... Mommy, when will I be five?"

"July fifteenth," she tells her.

"Right. I'll be five on July fifteenth, and then I get to go to big girl school."

"Big girl school? Really? That sounds pretty cool."

She nods. "Yep. I'm growing up," she says.

"Don't grow up too fast. Mommy wants you to be little as long as you can," Larissa tells her.

"Nope. Imma eat all my pizza and grow big and strong."

"Here you go. What do you say to Easton?" Larissa asks, setting her own cheese pizza in front of her.

"Thank you, East," she says, then looks down at the small pizza box in front of her. "This is mine?" she asks.

"Sure is." I ruffle her hair. "Water or milk to drink?"

"Milk," she says, picking up her first slice and taking a huge bite. She has sauce all over her face.

I watch as Larissa smiles down at her, reaching over with a napkin, wiping her face, then handing Paisley a new one. "Use this, please."

Paisley's head bobs up and down as she takes another bite, just as big as the first, covering her face once again in sauce. This time Larissa just grins and takes a bite of her own. It hits me that this feels right. Having them here, in my home, bringing it to life. I can only hope this is the beginning of many more nights I get to spend with them.

"That was a big pizza but it was little," Paisley says, leaning back in her chair. Her face is smeared with sauce where she attempted to wipe it with a napkin. She also has a small ring of milk framing her top lip, and her hands are on her belly.

"Come here, you." Larissa already has a wet paper towel in her hand, ready to clean her up. "Is your belly full?"

"So, so full," she replies dramatically.

"You girls want to watch a movie?"

"Oh, do you have *Pocahontas*? She's my favorite. Well, I like Cinderella and Belle, and—" Larissa places her hand over her mouth to stop her.

"P, I'm not sure Easton has princess movies."

"East, do you have princess movies?"

"No, sweetheart, but I'm going to have to fix that, huh?"

"Yeah, or I can bring mine next time I come over. I have lots of them."

"Well, how about we pull up Netflix and see what we can find?"

"Deal." She turns in her chair and holds her arms out for me.

"Paisley, you're a big girl, you can walk," Larissa chastises.

"But my East is so, so strong, and he can carry me."

I bite back my grin as I reach for her and place her on my hip. "Let's go, Momma. Time to find a movie."

"Let me clean up first," she says.

"Nope. It's an easy cleanup. I'll do it later. Now we relax."

"Yeah, Mommy, now we relax," Paisley repeats as I sit her on the couch. She moves over to the middle and pats the spot next to her. "I get to sit by Mommy and East." She smiles her adorable little smile that reaches in and grabs hold of my heart.

"Look, Paisley, *Pocahontas*," I say as I flip through the channels. She claps her hands and shocks me when she climbs up in my lap. She's sitting sideways with her head resting on my shoulder. Larissa opens her mouth, I assume to tell her to sit back on the couch, but I hold my hand up to stop her. "She's good. Now, you should move over here with us."

"Yeah, Mommy," Paisley chimes in.

Larissa moves over to sit next to me. Her shoulder bumping mine. Reaching out, I place my arm around her shoulder and bring her in close. I then relax into the couch and settle in for some Disney with both my girls in my arms.

Right where they should be.

We're barely a few minutes into the movie and Paisley is sound asleep. "I should take her home," Larissa whispers.

"Stay."

"It's close to her bedtime anyway."

Just a little longer. "I feel like I've barely seen you today and I'm going to be gone the next two days."

"I like to keep her to a routine. She does well with structure and needs a good night's sleep."

Turning my head, my lips meet her temple. "I'll walk you out." She slides out from underneath my arm and stands. I do the same, careful not to wake the sleeping princess in my arms. I manage to get her strapped into her car seat without waking her up.

"Once she's out, she's down for the night," Larissa says from behind me.

"She's a good kid." I don't know why I say it; it's not like we're talking about her behavior, but for some reason, it feels like it's important she hears that. "You've done a great job raising her."

Tears well in her eyes. "She's my entire world, Easton. She's already so attached to you...." Her voice trails off.

"Just her?" I ask, wrapping my arms around her waist and pulling her close.

"Not just her," she confesses.

I want to scream at the top of my lungs that they're mine. I want the world to know, but I settle for an internal fist bump, playing it cool. "Good." I kiss her forehead. "I'm attached too, Ris. This house, it's quiet. It's simply a place for me to sleep. With the two of you here, it's like you bring life to the place. It's something I didn't know I was missing."

"The novelty will wear off."

"Hey." With my index finger, I lift her chin. "This isn't because the two of you are new and shiny. It's here." I lay my hand over my chest. "I've enjoyed every minute that I've shared with the two of you, separate and together," I add, just for clarification. "We can ease her into the idea of us being more at your pace. I won't force your hand, but Larissa, we are more. More than I ever imagined I would want, and more than I could ever hope for. You might as well go ahead and get on board with that."

"And if I don't?" she asks. There's a sparkle in her eyes.

Bending, I press my lips to hers. "You will," I murmur as my mouth fuses with hers. Instead of words, I let my mouth convince her.

"Got it," she whispers as I pull away from the kiss.

I can't help but chuckle. "Good to know. Be careful driving home, babe. Call or text me when you get there so I know you're safe."

"I'm a big girl, Easton. I've been doing things on my own for a long time now."

"I know that. But you don't have to, not anymore. Drive safe," I say, stepping back and opening her door for her. For a minute, she just stands there staring up at me. No words are spoken and her facial expression is blank. It's like she's checked out. As she processes what I just said, I start to panic that I went too far, when a slow grin tips her lips.

"Do you always get your way?" she asks.

I shrug. "I always fight for what I want."

"And that's me?" I can hear the disbelief in her voice.

"That's you and your daughter." Seeing I've rendered her speechless, I shut her door and smile. She just shakes her head, the same smile playing on her lips as she hits the remote on her visor for the garage door and backs out. I watch her until I can no longer see her before closing the door and heading inside to get my phone. Stripping down to my boxer briefs, I climb into bed and wait to hear that they made it home okay.

CHAPTER 22
Larissa

I WAKE TO THE SOUND of my daughter's voice. I open my eyes and try to focus on where it's coming from and what she's saying.

"She's sweeping," I hear her say. "You gots a game today?" There's a pause. "You're going to be on TV?" she says, her four-year-old voice full of awe. "You'll have to tell my mommy that. I can't tell time yet."

I stifle my laugh. "Paisley," I say, causing her to jump.

She whips her head around to look at me from her spot on the floor just beside my bed. "She's awake, East. Tell her about the TV so I can watch you." She then pulls the phone from her ear, and hands it to me, just to take it back. She lifts it back to her ear. "Bye, East!" She yells too loudly as if she needs to in order for him to hear her, then hands the phone to me. This time, I'm able to grab it from her hands.

"Hello."

"Morning, beautiful."

"Morning," I say over a yawn. "Aren't you supposed to be on a flight?

"We're getting ready to board now. I just wanted to call and say good morning to my girls."

Thousands of butterflies flap their wings, ready to take flight in my belly. "You practice today?"

"Nah, not really. We'll stretch, watch some film, but that's about it. Our game is tomorrow night. Coach has us going a day early so we're not jet lagged from traveling."

"More time away," I say aloud without thinking.

"Yeah," he agrees. "I can say it never bothered me until now."

"Really?" I ask.

"I've never really had anyone to miss before. Sure, there's my family, and I miss them, but I don't see them every day. But with you and Paisley, it's... different."

Those damn butterflies are wreaking havoc. I don't know what to say to that. Well, I do, but blurting out those three little words over the phone isn't the way I want to do it. "Stay safe and have a good game." I know it's a shitty thing to do, to ignore his declaration, but that's the only other thing I can come up with right now.

He chuckles. "Ris, I'm going to talk to you again before the game."

My face heats, and I'm relieved he's not here to witness it. "I just know you're busy and I don't want to distract you."

"Baby, you're not a distraction. Well, you are, but in a good way," he says with a laugh.

"Well, have a safe flight," I amend.

He chuckles. "I'll call you girls when I land."

"Mommy, I wanna say some*fing*," Paisley says.

"Hold on a sec, East. P wants to talk to you."

"East, have a safe flight, bye," she says before handing the phone back to me.

"She's something else," he says with laughter in his voice.

"That she is."

"Bye, Ris, I'll talk to you soon," and with that, the line goes dead.

"Mommy, East is gonna be on TV. Did he tell you? Did he?" Paisley asks excitedly.

"He did. But Mommy has to work and it might be past your bedtime. Why don't we record it and we can watch it the next day?"

"Will I get to see him?"

"You will. We can watch it together the next day. I'm off work all day."

"Yay!"

I'm lucky my daughter is so easygoing. It's easy to steer her through the process from watching the game to helping me make breakfast. Paisley helps me make waffles for breakfast. She likes to hit the button on the toaster—this momma has no time for the homemade version. Maybe one day when I work a normal shift, but right now, the task sounds exhausting. Just as I'm placing the last dish in the dishwasher from breakfast, my cell phone rings. I groan when I see it's work, but answer anyway.

"Hello."

"Hey," Chloe greets me, "we're slammed, and Tina called in. Anyway, can you start your shift early? I told boss man I would call. Thought you might be more apt to say yes if I was the one who was asking." Chloe chuckles. "Not to mention, I thought maybe you could use the hours."

"We just finished breakfast. I need to call Mom and make sure it's okay to drop P off early and get ready. I'll text you."

"Thanks, gotta run," Chloe says, and ends the call.

"Paisley, run upstairs and wash your face and start brushing your teeth." Even as I say the words, I know I'll regret it from the mess that is sure to be in the bathroom. "Mommy has to go to work early."

"Okay," she says, knowing that arguing will do no good. We can use the extra money for sure. Her birthday is coming up, and regardless, we can always use the extra cash. That's the life of a single mom. I hate that my time with her is cut short. I console myself knowing she'll be with my mom, who dotes on her. They always have fun together.

Tapping on Mom's contact, I place my phone on speaker and begin to pick up the house a little. That was on today's agenda.

"Good morning," Mom says cheerily.

"Hey, Mom. I hate to ask, but can you take P early? I got called into work."

"Of course I can. I'm home, so come on over."

My mother is a saint. I would have been lost these past few years without her. "Thank you. I'm sorry."

"Don't be. You're doing all you can to take care of the two of you. I'm so proud of you, honey. I'll see you in a bit."

"Thanks, Mom." Hitting End, I dash to my room, passing P's door. She's dressing herself and I have to stifle a laugh. She has on blue jean shorts, a tutu in a rainbow of colors over the top, and a tank top. It's easier to let her go. I'll pack her a bag of other options in case Mom wants to go somewhere. I'm sure she has clothes there too. I race to my room and grab my uniform, then head back across the hall to shower. "Paisley, I'm getting in the shower. Stay in your room. Do not answer the door."

"Okay, Mommy," she replies. I leave the bathroom door open and strip down, stepping under the spray before it's even warm.

I've mastered the art of quick showers being a single mom. When P was a baby, I never wanted to leave her unattended for long. Even though she was strapped in her seat or later in her playpen in the bathroom. I opt to braid my wet hair as it saves so much time and keeps it out of my face when serving. I stop by Paisley's room on the way back to my bedroom to get my shoes and she's sitting on her bed, talking on the phone.

"Yeah, so I gots to go to Grams." I hear her say.

"Paisley Gray, who are you talking to? You know not to answer my phone," I scold her.

"I know, Mommy, but it's East. His picture popped up, and it's been so, so long since I talked to him." She holds the phone away from her ear and shows me the screen. All I can see is his name.

Walking into her room, I stop just beside her bed and hold out my hand. "Tell Easton goodbye and go pack whatever toys you want to take with you. We leave in ten minutes." I wait for her to tell Easton goodbye before she hands me the phone. "Go," I say in my stern mom voice. That snaps her into action, and she's rushing down the hall to get her bag.

"Hey," I say into the phone.

"You sound stressed, babe."

"Work called me in early, so I'm rushing to get there. I take it you just landed?"

"Yeah. We're getting ready to board the bus to take us to the hotel."

"I'm glad you had a safe flight. I hate to cut this short, but I really need to go so I can finish getting P ready and get her to Mom's."

"Call me tonight if you get time, or when you get home."

"Easton, it's going to be late. You have a game tomorrow."

"And I won't sleep unless I know you made it home okay."

"I'm a big girl, Easton."

"I know you are. You're also beautiful, and the best mommy to that little girl. But it's time to let someone worry about you. So call me. Please," he adds.

"Okay," I agree, because how do I argue with that? I've been doing it all on my own, with only my mom's help.

"Drive safe, babe. Give Princess P a hug from me."

I can't help but smile at his request. "I can do that."

"Bye, Ris."

"Bye, East." I end the call, holding my cell to my chest. Closing my eyes, I take a deep breath. I'm in so deep with him. His words, he's so confident about what he wants, and by pure luck, it's me and my daughter. I still worry, but we're getting closer every day. I don't worry so much for our broken hearts, mine and Paisley's, because I can't help but think that maybe just maybe, if this were to end, his might be broken too.

CHAPTER 23
Easton

T HIS IS THE FIRST ROAD trip where I can't wait to get home. I've gotten used to being gone more than I am home; it's the lifestyle of a professional baseball player. However, this time, this time there's something, or two someone's waiting at home for me, and I can't get there fast enough. Hence the reason why our flight landed forty minutes ago and instead of heading home, I'm headed to them, to my girls. I texted Larissa to let her know my flight landed. She's home today and said she and P are getting ready to settle in and watch last night's game.

I pull up outside her house, her SUV is in the driveway, and although I've never spent a single night here, it feels like home. I didn't tell Larissa I was coming. I didn't want to give her the opportunity to tell me not to. Grabbing their surprise, I climb out of my truck and stride toward the front door. I knock twice and wait. I hear Paisley yell out that there's someone at the door, then Larissa telling her to wait for her.

When the door opens, Paisley cheers and wraps her arms around my legs, and Larissa, her eyes are soft as she smiles at me. Leaning in, I kiss the corner of her mouth. I know I should worry about Paisley seeing, but I can't stop myself. It's not like this is the first time she's seen me kiss her. Larissa is gorgeous in a pair of what looks like sweatpants that have been cut into shorts, and a T-shirt that hangs off her shoulder. Her hair is pulled up in some kind of twisted knot on the top of her head.

"You're beautiful," I tell her when her hand goes to smooth her hair that's knotted back. "These are for you." I hand her a bouquet of multi-colored daisies. "And these," I crouch down so I'm eye level with Paisley, "are for my princess." I hand her the smaller bouquet that the lady at the flower shop was nice enough to cut down for me.

"These are for me?" she asks, wide-eyed. "I never gots flowers before."

"These are all yours. Every princess deserves her own flowers."

Her mouth falls open, her eyes wide as she looks at me. "Are you a prince, East? Do princes play baseball?" she asks.

I throw my head back and laugh. "No, I'm not a prince, but that doesn't mean that you're not my princess. Now," I stand then reach down and pick her up, "I heard you ladies were watching some baseball. Mind if I join you?"

Paisley giggles. It's a sweet sound, one I'll never get enough of. "You're going to watch yourself, silly."

I don't tell her that the chances are I'll spend more time staring at her mother than watching the game. "Doesn't matter who we watch as long as I get to hang out with you."

She places one of her hands on my cheek. "I like it when we hang out with you. Mommy said after I had to take a nap. Can you nap with me?" she asks.

"Paisley—" Larissa starts, but I cut her off.

"You know I love me some naps, P." I tweak her nose, and her face lights up.

"Come on in." Larissa steps back and opens the door for me. "I was just making popcorn. What would you like to drink?"

"Water's fine," I say. "Let's go help Mommy get these in water."

"I want mine in my room. Can I, Mommy?" she asks.

"Sure, P. Let's get them in some water first."

I follow Larissa into the kitchen and sit Paisley down on the counter. "What can I do?" I ask.

Larissa opens the cabinet and pulls down two mason jars. "You can put the flowers in these and I'll start the popcorn."

"Can I help?" Paisley asks.

"Sure, but it's a really big job. You sure you're up for it?" I ask. Her head bobs up and down. "Okay, so it's really important, once I get water in the jars, to hold it really still. That way when I put the flowers in, it doesn't tip over."

"I can do that. I'm good at helping, right, Mommy?"

"You sure are." Larissa smiles over at her.

"All right. Here we go." Grabbing the smaller mason jar, I fill it halfway with water and place it on the counter next to Paisley. "Hold it still for me," I tell her.

She nods, her face as serious as I've ever seen her as she turns sideways on the counter and places both hands on the jar. I unwrap the flowers and place them in the jar. "You did it!" I say excitedly. Her sweet smile lights up my world.

"I'm real good at helping," she tells me again.

"That you are. Let's move this out of the way." I slide the jar she's still holding onto down the counter.

"Shew," she says, shaking out her hands as if she'd been holding onto the jar for hours. I guess in her four-year-old mind, it might as well have been.

"You ready for the other one?" I ask her.

She shakes out her hands and holds them up for me to see. "Ready."

I place the larger jar on the table. "I don't know how I would have done this without you," I tell her as she wraps her tiny hands around the jar.

"I know," she agrees, and I have to bite back my laugh.

Unwrapping the larger bouquet of flowers, I place them in the jar and then move it down the counter next to the other one. I hold my hand up for a high-five, and she slaps hers into mine. "Great job."

"I'm ready to rewax," she says dramatically.

"Let's do this." I hold out my arms, and she leans into me. Settling her on my hip, I grab the three waters sitting on the counter and head to the living room. I drop Paisley onto the couch. Not hard enough she could get hurt, just enough that she bounces and cackles with laughter. I settle in, and she scoots up next to me.

"Look at you two all snuggled," Larissa says a few minutes later, joining us with a large bowl of popcorn.

"We worked hard," Paisley tells her. "We needed to rest."

Larissa laughs. "I bet."

What else do you say to an adorable four-year-old? You agree with them. "Let me take that." I reach for the popcorn.

"I can hold it. I'm in the middle, and we can share like a family."

I know it's all kinds of wrong, but I love it when she calls us a family. I'm sure Larissa is freaking the hell out, concerned we're moving too fast, but I'm not afraid of it. In fact, the sooner she hops on the speeding train, the better. "Ready for some baseball?" I ask. I want to hug her and tell her that I would be honored to be her family. To step in and fill the shoes of the father she lost before she even had a chance to meet him. I bite my tongue and pretend as if her comment didn't faze me, when in reality it's all that keeps running through my mind. I know it's going to take time for Larissa to get to where I am, but damn if I wish it would happen already.

Not ten minutes into the game and Paisley is over it. "When do I get to see you again, East?" she asks.

Glancing at the TV, I see where we are in the line-up. "I was already at bat, so it's going to be a minute. This innings dragged on. It's a few minutes," I say, trying to appease her.

"Maybe we should watch a princess movie instead. I get to see you now."

"Paisley," Larissa scolds her.

"It's fine," Reaching around Paisley, I place my hand on her shoulder. "A princess movie is fine with me."

"Actually, it's nap time," Larissa says.

"Aww, Mom, do we have to? East just got here."

"Yes, we do have to. You have practice tonight."

"Okay. East, will you lie down with me?"

"Sure, kiddo." I stand from the couch and stretch. When I turn around, Larissa's eyes are on my waist where my shirt has lifted, and Paisley is holding her arms in the air for me to pick her up.

"You can walk, P," Larissa reminds her.

"I know, but East is so, so tall. I like it when he carries me."

"Where do princesses takes naps?" I ask her.

"In my room, silly," she laughs.

"Oh, yeah, can you show me?" My eyes dart around the room, taking in their space. I can see so much of Larissa's personality from the color on the walls to the pillows on the couch. There are baskets of toys in every corner, telling me this house is lived in. It's a home. Something mine is missing.

She points down the hall and we head that way. When we get to her room, there are posters of all the Disney princesses on her walls. "That's my daddy. He's in heaven," she says, pointing to a picture on her nightstand.

"You know what that means, right?"

"That he's up there." She points to the ceiling. "But I can't see him. Momma says that's not how it works."

I swallow the lump in my throat. This little girl has my heart. "That's right, but that also means that your daddy is now your guardian angel. Do you know what that is?"

"He's an angel?" she whispers.

"He is. He's looking over you. So no matter if you are having a good day or a bad dad, he's always watching you."

"I wish I had a daddy here," she says, hugging her unicorn shaped pillow to her chest. It takes everything in me not to tell her that I'll be her daddy. Fuck, I'd be honored for her to call me Dad. "Will you read me a story, East?"

"How about I make one up?"

"Yes!" she cheers.

"Climb in," I say, holding the covers back for her, thankful we've moved on to lighter conversation.

"When I get big, I'm not taking naps."

"No? Naps are good for you. They give your body new energy so you can run and play."

"Are you taking a nap too?"

"I took one on the plane," I lie. It's just a small white lie, but I need some time with her momma. "I promise to be here when you wake up." I'm hoping Larissa doesn't kick me out before then.

"Are you coming to my practice?"

"We'll have to ask your mom and see if it's okay." I want to tell her I'll be at every single practice I can make it to, but I know that's crossing the line.

"Story," she reminds me.

"Right. Once upon a time, there was this beautiful princess, her name was Clarissa."

"That's like my mommy's name," she points out.

"I know." I wink at her.

"Clarissa and her daughter—"

She interrupts me before I can go on. "Paisley!" She giggles.

"Maisley," I correct her, causing her to laugh. I have no idea if it's a real name, but it rhymes with Paisley so I'm going with it. "Anyway, Maisley and her mom, Clarissa—"

She cuts me off again. "Maisley and her mommy, Clarissa, were living without a daddy," she says, breaking my damn heart.

"Hey, whose story is this, mine or yours?"

"I'm helping. I'm so, so good at it," she says.

"Okay, go on," I say, even though I'm not sure my heart can take it. Not where this little girl is concerned.

"Maisley and her mommy didn't have a daddy. One day, Maisley meets," she stops. "What whimes with East?"

"Beast?" I ask, seeing the *Beauty and the Beast* poster on her wall.

"Yeah!" she says like it's the best idea she's ever heard. "One day, Maisley meets Beast, and he becomes her friend."

"This story sounds awfully familiar," I say, tapping the end of her nose.

"East, I'm telling a story. You're 'posta stay quiet."

"Sorry, carry on." I hold my hands up in surrender.

"They play catch together, and take naps. Maisley loves her new friend so, so much, the end," she says proudly.

Leaning in, I brush her hair back from her eyes. "Can I tell you a secret?"

Her eyes grow wide and she nods. "I love you, too," I say, kissing the tip of her nose.

Her little arms fly around my neck and she squeezes me with all her might. "You're my best friend," she whispers.

I hold her a little tighter than I should with her size, but I need a minute for the emotions, the happiness, the love, the want, to flow through me. "All right you," I say once I've composed myself. "It's nap time. I'll be here when you wake up."

CHAPTER 24
Larissa

S TANDING OUTSIDE PAISLEY'S ROOM, I wipe the tears that I
can't keep from falling. He's so good with her, and she loves
him. Hearing their story is like someone reached inside my
chest and is squeezing my heart. I want to give her that. A family,
a man she can confide in, a man she can lean on. Until Easton,
there has been no one. At least not that she's met. I've had a few
dates here and there, but nothing and no one I would consider
bringing into her life. Why did I do it with him? I've asked myself
this question more times than I count, but it's not until now that
I can give myself an honest answer. Easton Monroe is a gift to
us. He's loving and kind. He makes our lives better by just being
a part of them.

"Hey," he says, stepping out into the hall. I don't have time to
turn and hide my tears before his big hands are cupping my
cheeks. "What's wrong?"

"She loves you."

"The feeling's mutual. She's a great kid."

"What are we doing, Easton? The more time you spend with her, the harder she falls for you. Her story—" My voice trails off and I shake my head.

"I can't tell you what you're doing, but I can tell you what I'm doing." He pauses, waiting for me to look at him. When my eyes are locked on his, he moves on. "I met this woman... she's gorgeous. I mean 'take my breath away' gorgeous. She's also smart as hell, hard-working, and somehow balancing working and school. She's cast a spell on me, so much so that I can't get her out of my head. A spell so profound that I don't even want to. Then, one day I find out she has a kid. A little girl, who resembles her momma is so many ways. A little girl who is living, breathing proof of how amazing this woman is. She's raised her with little help, supports both of them, and never once have I heard her complain about being tired or being ready to give up. Instead, I get this woman, who makes me want to be a better man, for her and her daughter."

Tears fall silently down my cheeks. I can feel them as they slide over his fingers that are still holding my face.

"I'm not playing games with you or with her. I know my lifestyle can be a pain in the ass, and it's not for everyone, but I'm asking you, Larissa. Please, let me in. Let's make us official. I want to be able to call you mine. I want to know that I can stop by to see the two of you whenever I want. I want you to do the same at my place, even if I'm not there. Take P swimming or just be there, in my space. I want our lives so entwined that none of us will be able to remember what life was like before we met."

I stand there, my mind racing to process his words. Closing my eyes, I take a deep breath and release the worry and the fear. This man is standing before me, pouring his heart out. He wants to be here, or he wouldn't be before me now. I know that. He's great with my daughter, and if the day comes where this doesn't work, she will know the love of a good man. Something she's never experienced. I know in my heart that's what he is: a good man.

"What do you say, Ris? Can we make this thing between us official?"

Slowly, I open my eyes. He's watching me, waiting for my answer. I can't seem to find the words, and a lame head nod doesn't seem to be fitting for this moment. It needs more. So I stand on my tiptoes and press my lips to his. Before I realize what's happening, Easton grips my ass and lifts me into the air. On instinct, I wrap my legs around his waist, and lock my arms around his neck, holding on for the ride. He doesn't stop until we're in my room across the hall. Easton breaks the kiss and sits me on the bed. I watch him as he walks back out the bedroom door. I can hear his footsteps throughout the house. I'm just about to go look for him to see what he's doing when he appears in my doorway. Quietly, he closes the door and turns the lock.

"What did you do?"

"I locked the front door and moved the couch in front of the hallway."

"O-kay," I say slowly. "I get the front door. Why the couch?"

"Because I'm going to devour you and if we happen to not hear Paisley wake up, I don't want her to get burned in the kitchen, or get cut, or sneak out the front door or anything else curious little girls can get into."

I try to hold back my laughter, but fail. "She knows the rules. You didn't have to go to that extreme," I say as I splutter with laughter.

"She's not getting hurt on my watch," he grumbles. He stalks toward me, leaning over the bed and pressing his lips to mine. "I take care of what's mine," he says before kissing me again, pushing his tongue past my lips. Leisurely, he strokes my tongue with his, reminding me of our one and only night we've spent together. "Tell me what you want, Ris."

"You." He moves to stand between my legs, and I can feel how ready he is through my thin cotton shorts.

"Tell me what we are." His lips venture across my cheek and down my neck. "Tell me we're official."

"We don't have to be to do this," I remind him.

He stops, pulling away his eyes to find mine. "Yeah, in fact, we do. I'm not playing games here, Larissa. I meant every word I said. I want to take us beyond the bases, baby."

My heart's racing but I'm not sure if it's from him and his touch, his tender kisses against my heated skin, or if it's from the words about to come out of my mouth. "We're official."

"Yeah?" he asks, his dark eyes sparkling.

I nod.

"Can we tell Paisley? I don't want to hide this from her. I'm just as enamored with her as I am you."

She's already attached to him; I've let that happen. What's the point in holding out on him now? "Yeah, we can tell her."

He crashes his lips to mine. "Need you now." His hands go to my shorts and he begins to work them over my hips. I lift, making it easier for him. Once he slides them down my legs, panties and all, he tosses them on the floor. "How long does she nap?"

"We don't have much time," I pant. Her naps are shorter and less frequent the older she gets. I have a feeling I would have had more of a fight on my hands if it weren't for Easton telling her naps were good.

"Then I better get to work." Stepping back, I watch as he unbuckles his shorts, pulls a condom from his pocket, then grips and tugs down his shorts, along with his boxer briefs to the floor. My eyes are glued to him as he strokes himself. "Like what you see?" he asks.

"Meh, you know how to work that thing?" I ask, and he looks horrified at the question.

"Really, Larissa?" He's stroking himself with one hand and running his fingers through my folds with the other.

"I think you should show me," I say, raising a brow in challenge.

He laughs and shakes his head. "I'll show you." He reaches for the condom.

"You had me pegged as a sure thing?"

"No." He shakes his head vehemently. "I just wanted to be prepared. I know I can't keep my hands off you, and on the slim chance we were able to end up in this very spot, I wasn't letting something like protection keep me from being inside you again." Quicker than I anticipated, he has the condom on and is bracing his hands beside me on the bed. "You're gonna need to be quiet," he says.

I'm just about to tell him that Paisley can sleep through anything, when he pushes inside me. My hands grip his back and my eyes close. I bite down on my bottom lip to keep from crying out. She can sleep through anything, but I definitely want her to sleep through this.

Easton smiles down at me and then swivels his hips. "You still think I don't know how to use my... bat?" he asks, smirking.

"Mmm, the jury's still out," I manage to groan, goading him. I know damn good and well he knows how to use what the good Lord gave him. My taunting spurs him on as he lifts my legs and sets one on each of his shoulders. Gripping my hips, he begins a relentless pace. Over and over, he thrusts inside me, and all I can do is hang on for the ride.

"C-close," I pant, my orgasm looming. He takes that as his cue to roll his hips and speed his thrusts all at the same time. I'm not quite sure what's going on, but whatever he's doing, I don't want him to stop.

Ever.

My nails dig into his skin and my orgasm crashes over me. "I'm with you, baby," I hear him say, and then there's nothing but ringing in my ears as pure bliss takes over my body. Easton is only the second man I've ever been with, and nothing in my past compares to what just happened. Well, unless you count our first time together. Actually, any time with him always feels better than the time before. He's magical that way. Then again, maybe it's us. Maybe we're magical together.

My eyes are closed, my breathing labored as I release my grip on him and let my hands fall to my sides. He settles on the bed next to me, legs hanging off the side. I can't speak. Hell, I can't move. I'm just soaking up the rush. I should probably say something, thank him for the best orgasm of my life, but speaking takes too much effort. Instead, I move my hand, seeking him out. When I feel him, I link my fingers through his and hold on tight.

"I've got you, Ris." His warm breath hits my ear.

Cracking open one eye, I see him leaning on his elbow looking down at me. "There she is," he whispers. "I missed you," he teases.

"You tried to kill me," I quip.

He chuckles, low and deep. "Death by orgasm. What a way to go." Slowly, his soft yet firm lips press against mine. Just as I'm about to beg him for round two, I hear the pitter-patter of little feet and then the bathroom door close.

Easton jumps up, disposes of the condom in the trash can beside the nightstand and is dressed in what seems like ten seconds. I can't hold back, and laughter bubbles out of me. I think he's moving faster than he does on the field. His coach would be proud. He winks at me, not at all fazed by my laughter, then slips out the door. I clean up the best that I can without the bathroom, and quickly get dressed. When I open my bedroom door, I hear laughter in the kitchen. Not sure what I'll find, I take small steps seeing what I can hear.

"Did you ask my mommy about my practice. I really want you to go," Paisley asks him.

"Your mom and I talked and I'm going to be at as many practices and games that I can. In fact, anytime you want me there, as long as I'm not at work, I'll be there."

"Really? Just like the other daddies? He's up there, remember?" she asks him, and I can picture her pointing to the sky.

I've tried my best to keep the memory of Steven alive for her, but it's hard to explain to a four-year-old what heaven is and why she never got to meet her father.

"Your daddy loved you very much," he tells her. I can hear the emotion in his voice.

"How do you know? Did you know my daddy?" she asks him.

"No, but I know because you are a princess and all daddies love their princesses."

I'm about to be a blubbering mess. Taking a deep breath, I school my features and join them in the kitchen. "Hey, you two." I stop and kiss P on top of the head. "How was your nap?"

"So, so good. I told East a story and it was eshosting," she says dramatically.

"Exhausting," I correct her. Easton is standing by the stove, arms and legs crossed, shaking with laughter. "Let's get you some dinner, and then we'll head to practice."

"How about we go out to dinner?" Easton offers.

"I can make something," I tell him.

"I know, but I kinda want to take my girls out." He shrugs. "You agreed and I kind of want to show you off." I know what he's asking. Am I ready to be in the limelight as his girlfriend? I'm shocked that I do. I have no worries when it comes to how he feels for me. It's a new feeling, but a welcome one all the same.

"Show what off?" Paisley asks.

"I want to show you this diner that my family and I have been going to since I was about your age," he tells her.

"Yay! Can we, Mommy? Please, oh pretty please?"

Looking over at Easton, my eyes narrow on his pouting bottom lip, which is stuck out dramatically. "Pretty please, Mommy?" he asks.

"You know, you shouldn't stick your lip out like that. A bird could poop on it," I tell him.

Paisley giggles. "Don't worry, East. She tells me that too and it's never happened. Mommy's just joking."

"Good to know," he tells her. "So how about it? Can I take you ladies out for dinner?"

"Yeah," I agree. I look at Paisley. "Let's get you changed and get your stuff together for practice."

"Woohoo!" She jumps off the kitchen chair and rushes off down the hall to her room.

"This is us going out in public, Ris. The paparazzi are going to see you and her. They're going to know you're mine. You okay with that?"

"Yeah, but I worry about her. I want her to be safe."

"I would never let anything happen to either one of you. It's pretty chill here. People are used to seeing the Blaze players out and about. Just know that it's going to be front page news."

"Oh yeah? Why's that?" I counter.

"The Tennessee Blaze's most eligible bachelor, voted two years in a row, is now off the market," he says, walking toward me. He stops, bends down, and kisses the corner of my mouth. I wait for the panic, but it never comes. I'm happy, Paisley is happy, and Easton, well, if the smile he's giving me is any indication, he's happy too. I'm excited to see what's yet to come.

"Ready," Paisley says, sliding into the room in her socked feet.

"Hold up, slugger. Let's get your shoes on while your mom checks to make sure we have everything." He pops her onto the counter, takes her shoes from her and proceeds to place them on her feet and tie them as if he's done this with her a thousand times.

Easton Monroe is indeed a good one. One who has already captured my heart.

CHAPTER 25
Easton

W E HAVE A HOME GAME today and I'm stoked that Larissa and Paisley are going to be here. Last night I stopped by and dropped them off some T-shirts with the Blaze logo on the front, and *Monroe* and *20*, my number, on the back. Hell, it turns me on knowing Larissa is wearing my name and number, and Paisley... pride thrums through me that my little princess will be cheering me on.

We had a mandatory team meeting, which means I had to be here extra early, so the girls are coming on their own. I hate that. I wanted to pick them up and show them around the stadium before it starts to fill up. Next time I'll make it happen, because there will definitely be a next time.

"What's got you staring at your phone?" Drew asks, leaning over my shoulder.

"Nothing, man. Ris said she would text me when she gets here and so far, nothing."

"I'm sure she'll be here," he says, taking his seat beside me in front of his locker. "How are things going there? I feel like you never go out with us anymore. Away games, you rush back to your room, and when we're home, you're missing too."

"Couldn't be better," I tell him honestly. "I'm crazy about her, about both of them."

He nods. "Am I going to have to ask Larissa for permission for you to come hang out with the boys?" he jokes.

"Nope. I don't need permission. I'd just rather be with them right now. Traveling takes so much time away, and when we go on long stretches on the road, it's going to be hard to be away from them."

"She hooked you." He smirks.

"They both did." Just as the words leave my mouth, my phone vibrates and a picture of the three of us that we took at the zoo, lights up my screen. "Hey, babe, you guys here?"

"About that," she sighs, "we can't make it."

"What? Why? What's going on?" I fire off questions. I was really looking forward to them coming today.

"P isn't feeling well. She was complaining of her throat bothering her last night, then didn't say anything else this morning. I thought maybe it was just allergy drainage. She started running a low-grade fever about an hour ago. I gave her some medicine to bring it down, and she's snuggled up on the couch watching *Pocahontas*."

"Can I talk to her?"

"Sure."

I wait as she hands the phone to Paisley.

"East," she croaks into the phone, and I feel like a dick for making her talk.

"Hey, princess. Don't say anything, I just wanted to tell you to feel better. I'll be right there as soon as my game's over."

"O-kay," she croaks.

"Give the phone back to Mommy." I hear shuffling while she gives the phone back to Larissa.

"Sorry—"

"Don't be sorry for being an incredible mother. I hate that she's sick and I'm stuck here. I'll be there as soon as the game's over."

"You don't have to do that. We can't risk you getting sick. You leave Tuesday for a week."

"All the more reason for me to be there. I need to see her. Do you girls need anything? What can I bring her?" I ramble on with questions before she has time to answer them.

"I was going to have Mom come stay with her so I could run out and get her some Popsicles and ice cream."

"I'll bring them on my way home."

"Easton, it's fine, really. We've got this."

"I know you do, but I want to help. You just cuddle with our girl and I'll be there soon."

"Okay. Have a good game."

"Thanks, babe." We end the call, and the urge to race out of the stadium and rush to them is strong. So damn strong I grip my phone in my hand, a war waging inside me. I know it's just a sore throat, but she's never been sick, not since I came in the picture and... I don't really know. I just feel like they need me.

"You good?" Drew asks.

"Paisley is sick, sore throat and a bit of a temperature. They're not coming."

"That sucks."

"Yeah," I say, still gripping my phone. Resting my elbows on my knees, I stare down at my cleats. How do the guys with families deal with this shit? My phone vibrates in my hand. Lifting my head to see who it is, I smile when I see Larissa's name.

Larissa:

We're okay here, Easton. You focus on the game.

Kick some Badger ass.

We'll be watching you on TV.

She knows me well enough to know I was thinking of saying fuck the game to go to them. It sounds ridiculous even to me. It's a sore throat. She knew what I needed to hear.

Mind reader?

Larissa:

Easton reader.

Ha ha. See you soon, baby.

Larissa:

We'll be here.

Stashing my phone in my locker, I finished getting suited up for the game. The sooner it starts, the sooner it ends and I can get to my girls. That's something I never thought I would feel when it came to baseball. Baseball has been my life since I was a kid. Meeting Larissa and Paisley changed my perspective on life. I make a great living and I've invested well. I'm set for life. I love the sport, but I love them more.

I freeze.

I love them.

Love her. I told Paisley I loved her since she's a cute kid and is hard not to love, but it's more than just she's cute. I love her.

It's that I want to be the man she depends on. I want to be the father figure in her life. And her mom, Larissa, I just want her. My heart wants her. My soul wants her. Every part of me wants her.

I love my girls.

CHAPTER 26
Larissa

P AISLEY IS OUT COLD BEFORE the game even starts. I've recorded it even though I watched. Maybe she and East can watch it together later. I know he's been teaching her about the positions and the rules of the game. Her attention span is short, but that doesn't seem to deter him.

Once the game ends, I fold the two loads of laundry I washed, dried, and then ignored as I didn't want to miss a glimpse of East. I'm just finishing putting away the final load when I hear his soft knock at the door. With a glance at the couch to see P is still sound asleep, I rush to the door to let him in.

I'm shocked at what I find. Easton Monroe, starting first baseman for the Tennessee Blaze, is on my front porch. Sure, he's my Easton too, but right now, he's in his dusty, dirty uniform, holding a grocery bag in each hand.

"Hey," I say, stepping back so he can come in.

"How is she?"

"Sleeping. I need to wake her in just a few to give her some more medicine for the fever."

"Do we take her to the emergency room?" he asks.

I fight back my smile at his concern. He's so ridiculously sweet. "No, I'll call to get her in with her pediatrician tomorrow. As long as the medicine keeps her fever down, we should be good. It will also help with the pain."

"I bought everything I thought she might want. If I forgot something, I can go back out."

"How about a shower? You could have done that at the stadium you know?"

"No time, I wanted to get here."

"Do you at least have a change of clothes with you?"

"Yeah, my bag is out in my truck."

I take a minute to look him over. He's a sweaty, dusty, gorgeous mess. "You went into the store like that?" I ask.

"Yeah, if I'd been thinking, I would have sent someone to do it during the game. Then I could have been here sooner."

"Easton," I say, reaching out and resting my hand against his chest. "We're fine. She's fine. She's sick, but kids get sick."

"Not ours," he says adamantly.

My mouth drops open at his reply. I try to speak, but the words just will not come. I try again, but don't get the chance when Paisley's croaking voice calls out for not me, but Easton.

"East," she croaks softly. I can hear the anguish in her voice.

Easton kicks off his cleats and rushes past me to the couch. "Hey, princess," he whispers. Bags still in his hands, he leans forward and places them on the table. "I got ice cream and Popsicles, some sherbet, all kinds of things that might make your throat feel better."

She opens her mouth to speak, and he hushes her. "Shh, P, just point to what you want and I'll get it for you."

I watch as she points to a Popsicle and he makes quick work of pulling out the flavors and having her point to the one she wants. No one has ever cared for her beside me and my mom. There's a lump in my throat watching him with her. He's gentle, and I can see the worry on his face. He's not used to kids. I know he has a sister who's a good bit younger than him, but I can imagine as a kid he didn't pay much attention. Yet here he is, tending to my daughter as if it's second nature. As if she is really his.

"You eat your Popsicle while I run and take a shower. Then we can snuggle, okay?" She bobs her head up and down when he's finished speaking. Leaning in, he kisses her forehead. "I'll be right back."

Standing from the couch, he walks toward me. "Hey, baby." He kisses the corner of my mouth. "Let me grab a shower and you can take a break." He gives me another quick kiss before he rushes out the door to get his bag.

I don't bother to correct him that I don't need a break. Paisley has slept most of the day, but the fact he wants to means something. It means everything. When he's here with us, he's not Easton Monroe, the baseball player. He's our East. He's the man who we both adore.

While Easton takes a shower, I grab a couple of paper towels. One I wet, the other I leave dry, and head back to the living room. "Use this for your hands." I hand Paisley the wet paper towel." Her lips and tongue are red from the cherry Popsicle. Her hands too.

I'm just taking a seat in the chair when Easton comes back into the room. His hair is still wet from his shower, and he's wearing gym shorts and a T-shirt. He walks to the couch and sits down, pulling P's legs into his lap.

"Is it yummy?" he asks.

She nods.

"Good game," I say, pulling his attention away from Paisley.

"Thanks. I was distracted and played like sh-crap, but thanks."

My lips twitch. "I didn't notice."

"I mean, it wasn't my worst game, but my mind was here, you know?"

"Sorry about that. I didn't want you to worry when we didn't show up, but it sounds like you worried regardless."

"Of course I did." He almost sounds offended. "You two are what matters, Larissa."

"All done," Paisley croaks.

I hop out of my seat, and help her clean up with the wet towel, then wipe her face and hands with the dry one. I feel her forehead and she's warm. "It's time for more medicine. I'll be right back."

"It's yucky," I hear her rasp out to Easton as I leave the room.

When I make it back to the living room, Paisley is curled up on Easton's lap with a blanket thrown over both of them. "Open up," I say, holding the medicine spoon out for her. She takes it and makes her usual face, letting me know she's not happy about it.

"Now, we watch a movie," Easton says, wrapping his arms around her and snuggling her close.

"Can we watch *Cinderella*?"

"Sure we can, sweet girl. Whatever you want."

I want to scold him for spoiling her, but she's sick, and honestly, even if she wasn't, I'm sure I would bite my tongue. He's so good with her, so much so my heart aches. She's never had this, a male role model, and she's soaking up time with him like a sponge. I still have the worry in the back of my mind, but seeing her with him, and him with her, no way can I deny them this.

I sift through the DVDs and find *Cinderella*, putting it in the DVD player and grabbing the remote.

"Come here, baby." Easton pats the cushion next to him where he still sits with Paisley on his lap. I go willingly and curl up into his side. I feel his lips press against the top of my head and bite back my smile. This, in this moment, I couldn't ask for more. Well, maybe for P to feel better, but the three of us like this... it's everything.

CHAPTER 27
Easton

"HEY, MAN, WE'RE ALL GOING out to breakfast. You in?" Fisher asks.

"Nah, thanks though."

"You're all domesticated and shit. Can't hang out with your boys?"

"Not today. Larissa's exhausted. She's picked up three extra shifts this week because one of her coworkers has been sick. Paisley had two games, from catching up with rain dates a couple of weeks ago, which means all five nights this week she or her mom has had to get her to a game or practice. I was out of town and couldn't help, so I'm going over there to see what I can do."

"She does it all on her own?" Carr asks, joining the conversation.

"Yeah, I mean her mom helps, but other than that, it's all Larissa."

"Where's the dad?" Fisher asks.

"Killed in the line of duty."

"Fuck," Drew mumbles under his breath.

"Yeah, she won't ask for help, but she's getting it."

"Let us know if we can help."

"Thanks, man. I'll catch you guys later." I grab my bag and head out to my truck. We were on the road this week for a seven-day stretch. This morning was a short team meeting and workout, and we're off until our game on Sunday. It doesn't take long to reach her place. When I walk up to the front door, I hear Paisley crying and Larissa telling her to go to her room. Quickly, I knock on the door, and it swings open a few minutes later to a frazzled Larissa.

"Hey," she says, stepping back to let me in.

"You okay?"

"Yeah, just trying to get things done. Paisley is wound for sound today."

"I heard her crying."

She sighs, her shoulder slumping in defeat. "Yeah, she insists on watching TV out here instead of in her room or mine, and she has to have it loud enough that I'm sure Mom can hear it at her place. I've had to repeatedly ask her to turn it down. I have a paper due by six tonight, and I need to concentrate."

I open my arms and she walks into them. I hold her close, my mind racing as to what I can do to help. That's when it hits me. "Go pack up your computer and whatever you need. You're coming to my place. Sit out by the pool or use my office, the couch, whatever you need. Just go and get your work done. If you do it here, you're just going to think about everything else on your list that you feel like you have to do today."

"I'm fine here."

"Nope. Go pack. I'm going to go get P, get her to pack some toys for later, but for now, she and I are going on a date."

"A date?" she asks. Her eyes, although filled with stress, are just a little brighter at my words.

"A date," I say again. "You're going to go to my place and forget about work, about laundry, and whatever else you are worrying about in that pretty little head of yours. The fridge is stocked. You go and get your work done. When you're finished, take a nap, take a swim, I don't care. P and I will be on a date."

"Easton," she says, but I stop her from continuing by placing my finger over her lips.

"Let me do this. Let me take care of you. This is what you need, Ris. Time to think, to get caught up with school."

"Just a couple of hours of focused time and I'll be done."

"Good. Then you can take the rest of the day for you. Relax, soak in the tub, read a book, go get a pedicure, whatever you want. I've got P. We'll meet you back at my place later today."

She opens her mouth then closes it again. When she finally finds her words, I'm shocked when she says, "I don't know what I would do without you."

Kissing her temple, I whisper, "You're never going to have to find out." Releasing her, I head toward Paisley's room. I find her on her bed with her arms crossed and a scowl on her face. "What's up, princess?"

"Mommy yelled at me."

"She did?" I act as if I have no clue what's going on.

"Yeah," she says angrily.

"You know what?"

"What?"

"Mommy's having a bad day. Do you ever have bad days?"

"Like when Gram says I can't have more cookies and they're so, so good?"

I fight my grin. "Yep. That makes you upset and causes you to have a bad day. Mommies have bad days too." I sit on her bed. "I have an idea. Mommy is working really hard this week at her job, picking up shifts, and she has a lot of schoolwork. How about you and I go spend the day together. Let Mommy have the house all to herself. It will be nice and quiet so she can focus."

"She told me to be quiet."

I nod. "Sometimes when you're really trying hard to concentrate on something, you need quiet."

"Where are we going?"

"I'm not sure yet. Let's get you a bag packed with some toys and a change of clothes, just in case. We'll go have some fun and meet Mommy back at my house later today."

"Can we swim?"

"Sure, P, just make sure you pack your bathing suit. Do you need any help?"

"Nope. I'm almost dis many." She holds up five fingers.

"That's right, you have a birthday coming up. Go get a bag packed. I'll be in the living room talking to Mommy."

"Okay!" she says excitedly, jumping off the bed. I watch her until I know she can reach her bag, which is located at the bottom of her closet, then leave her to pack.

"I take it she's excited?" Larissa asks.

"She sure is. She's packing a bag with toys, her swimsuit, and a change of clothes. You should do the same before you head to my place."

She nods. "Thank you, Easton. I'm failing at mom life this week."

"Hey." I lift her chin with my index finger so I can look at her. "You're not failing, baby. You're stressed. You've put in a lot of hours this week, and school is hectic. It's okay to ask for help. I'm here now. You don't have to do this on your own." Her answer is to stand on her tiptoes and press her lips to mine.

"Ready," Paisley says, dragging her bag that's stuffed full into the living room.

"Come here, P," Larissa calls her over. "Mommy's sorry for yelling. Will you forgive me?"

"East said you were so, so busy and needed quiet, so we're going out," she explains, as if the earlier incident never happened. This kid is a rock star.

"You be a good girl for East, okay?"

"I will." She turns and places her hand in mine. "Ready?" she asks, bouncing on the balls of her feet.

"Ready." I pick her up and place her on my hip. Grabbing her bag, I toss it over the opposite shoulder. "See you soon, Ris." I kiss her lips quickly, which has Paisley saying, "Eww cooties," making us both laugh.

With another round of hugs and goodbyes, I'm able to get Paisley strapped in her seat, and we're on the road. "What do you want to do today?" I glance quickly in the rearview mirror.

"Umm." She taps her index finger on her chin. "What do you want to do?"

"We can do anything. What do you do with your mom?"

"We usually go to the grocery store or the park. Sometimes we go shopping for clothes. We're gonna go soon. Mommy says I need new shoes."

"What kind of shoes?"

"The kind you tie. I don't know how to tie them yet, but my other ones are so, so small they hurted my feet. I don't need them until it gets cold," she explains. Something I'm sure Larissa has said.

"Well then, how about we head to the mall and get you some shoes?"

"Okay," she agrees. "Can we get a cookie from that place that smells so, so good. Sometimes Mommy and me stop there. We don't always, but they are so, so good," she says, trying to convince me.

What she doesn't realize is that I need zero convincing. No way can I say no to her. "Cookies it is." She fills the rest of the ride to the mall with chatter. She has one more game for her T-ball season and her birthday that's coming up in two weeks.

"What do you want for your birthday?" I ask as I help her unbuckle her car seat.

"Lots of stuff." She smiles as I place her on my hip. Sure, she can walk, but she won't be this little forever.

"What kind of stuff?"

"I want an American girl doll. They look just like me, and we can get matching clothes and everything, but they costs lots of dollars. Oh, and Build-A-Bear. Mommy says one day we will go there, too."

"What's Build-A-Bear?"

"East, it's so, so fun. You get to stuff your bear. You get to make it all by yourself and buy it clothes and stuff."

"Where is this Build-A-Bear place?"

She laughs. "It's here silly."

"Well, all right then. First thing's first, we get you shoes."

"Mommy don't buy my shoes here. We get them at the Walmarts."

"Well, today we're getting them from the mall." My heart squeezes in my chest for this little girl and her amazing mother. Larissa busts her ass to take care of Paisley and I'm sure goes without herself. Not anymore. I want to take care of both of them. I want to make it so Larissa doesn't have to work so hard, so that she can spend more time with her daughter. I want Paisley to have the toys that all the other kids have, the shoes that they have.

"Okay," she agrees, none the wiser.

The first store we go into I lead her back to the little girls' shoes, and she spots a pair of white Nikes with a pink swoosh. "Oh, those are really pretty," she says.

"You like those?"

"Yeah," she says, eyes wide.

"Can I help you, sir?" one of the store associates asks.

"Yes, we need to measure her to see what size she needs."

"Sure thing." He measures her foot, and we ask him for the pink Nikes in her size. "Here you go," he says, handing me the box.

I place P on the stool and slip off her sandal. "Put this sock on while I get the laces ready."

"Okay." She takes the sock, and with a look of pure concentration on her face, she pulls it on her foot. "I did it," she tells me.

"Great job, Princess. Now let's try this shoe." I put it on her foot and lace it up. "Can you walk that way for me so we can see how they feel?"

She nods, hops off the stool and walks up and down the row of shoes. "These are soft," she says.

"You like them? We can keep looking."

"No, I like these so, so much."

"All right, come over here and let me see where your toe is."

"East," she giggles loudly, "my toes are in my shoes." She laughs.

"Get over here, giggle box." When she's standing in front of me, I check her toes, and it's right on. "Can we get these in a half size bigger?" I ask the sales assistant.

"Why we doing that?" she asks. "These ones fit."

"Because you will grow between now and then. I want you to be able to wear them longer."

"I'm getting so, so big. My birthday I'll be this many." She holds up her hand, showing me five fingers.

"I know. Five years old, you're practically an old woman."

"No, that's Gram," she says seriously. I have to bite my tongue to keep from laughing.

After we pay for the shoes, I stop at the mall directory and look for this Build-A-Bear place. It's not too far down from the shoe store, so I head that way.

"You smell those cookies?" she asks me.

I smile down at her. "Sure do. How about we shop a little more, then grab some lunch? We'll save the cookies for dessert."

"Yay!" she cheers. "Can we take one to Mommy too.'

"Sure thing, princess." We continue walking in the direction of the bear place when Paisley stops and looks up at me. "What's up?" I ask her.

"Thank you so, so much for my shoes. I forgot to say that."

"You're welcome. Let's go see what else we can get into. Let's buy something for Mommy. You got any ideas?"

"I don't know. What do you think?"

"I think we should get her something she needs, like your shoes. Do you remember her saying anything that she would like to have?"

"Hmmm," she says, thinking.

"Shoes or clothes, something for school?"

"She was yelling at her computer today when I was being loud. It did something to her homework."

"What did it do?"

"She said it froze it. I don't know how that happened because it wasn't cold when I touched it, but then Mommy told me not to touch her computer. That it was on its last leg. I didn't tell her this 'cause she was already sad, but computers don't have legs. Not that I can see. Do computers have legs, East?" she asks.

"No, that's an expression people use when something is about to break forever."

"Oh," her mouth forms an O.

Looking up, we just happen to be standing in front of an Apple store. I know Larissa has an iPhone, so this should work great. Twenty minutes later, we have a new computer, with a pink case, that Paisley picked out, in hand.

"Now what?" she asks.

"Well, I have a surprise for you. It's this way," With her hand in one of mine, and our purchases in the other, we head toward Build-A-Bear. When we stop outside the store, she shrieks.

"East! Can we go here, can we?"

"This is your surprise."

"I love you," she says, launching herself at my legs and wrapping her arms around them, squeezing me tightly.

I see a few patrons raise their cell phones to get pictures. Her shriek must have tipped them off. Either that or someone from one of the other stores must have put it on social media that I was here. Ignoring them, I guide Paisley into the store. "Okay, princess, let's build that bear." We spend a few hours building the perfect bear and picking out accessories. We opt to get cookies to go, and grab something for us to eat at my place. She's exhausted and I get no arguments. Apparently, bear making makes you so, so tired. We make one more stop for some Bath & Body Works lotion and body spray for Larissa, then head home. We're barely out of the lot before she's fast asleep.

CHAPTER 28
Larissa

W HEN EASTON LEFT WITH PAISLEY, all I wanted to do was sit around and cry. My laptop, which is as old as I am—well not really, but I bought it used and it was outdated then— keeps freezing up. It's taking me more than double the time it should take to get these assignments in. To top it off, I yelled at my daughter and took my frustration out on her. I feel so damn guilty. I feel guilty that Easton has her for the day when I'm her mom. I should be able to handle this, but this week has been rough, and I just... lost it for a little bit.

Needing to get out of this house before I go stir crazy, I pack up my laptop and books, then pack a bag with my swimsuit, and some clothes. I throw in the essentials and something for Paisley as well. I know she packed her bag, but she's four. It's hard to tell what she put in that thing. At the time, I didn't care. I just needed a break. I hate that feeling. I love my daughter more than life, but damn, it felt like the walls were starting to crumble. Easton showed up just when we needed him.

That brings me to now. I'm sitting at Easton's dining room table, my laptop and books spread out, music playing on my phone, and a glass of wine in hand. I hesiatate before drinking it, knowing I need to drive us home later, but I know Easton will let us stay here, or drive us home. He's solid and dependable, and everything I could want in a man. That made it easy to fall head over heels in love with him. Too bad I'm too big a chicken to tell him.

I hear the garage door open and decide it's time for a break. My damn computer has been frozen in the same spot for the last fifteen minutes. I have to wait it out. Then I can type some more. Every time I save or get on the Internet while typing, it does this.

Standing, I meet them at the garage door. What I find melts my heart. Easton has a sleeping Paisley in his arms, rubbing her back as he carries her into the house.

"Hey, baby. You get any work done?" he whispers, taking P to the living room and laying her gently on the couch.

"Not really. Technical difficulties."

"I heard about that. I think I have a solution." He stops in front of me, bends and presses his lips to mine. "Be right back." I watch him go back out to the garage, only to come back in with his arms full of bags.

"What is all that?"

"We went shopping." He sets the bags on the opposite end of the dining room table from where I'm working. "This is for you." He hands me a Bath & Body Works bag. "This is also for you." He hands me a large bag from the Apple store.

"Easton?"

"I wanted to get you something that you've been needing to make things easier for you. P said you were yelling at your computer. She also said you mentioned it being on its last leg, but didn't want to tell you computers don't have legs because you were sad." He smiles.

"This is too much." This man with a heart of gold, how can I ever repay him for what he's given us? Not the gifts, but the steady shoulder to lean on, the laughs, the hugs, the kisses. If I didn't already, it would be impossible not to fall in love with him.

"It's not. I told you, Larissa, I want to take care of you. I have the means to do these things. What kind of boyfriend would I be if I knew you were struggling, spending hours more than necessary because your computer was shit, and could afford to make it better? That's what I'm doing."

"You make our lives better. You don't need to spend your money on us."

"Noted, but I'm going to regardless." He reaches out and cups my cheek. His thumb strokes gently. "I care about you, about both of you. I want to do this. I want to help."

I can feal the tears building. "Thank you, I'll pay you—" He cuts me off by pressing his lips to mine.

When he finally pulls away, his voice leaves no room for argument. "No, you will not. This was a gift to you. My girlfriend." He hands me the bag again. "Now, open it and set it up, so you can kick this assignment's ass. While you're doing that, I'll show you what else we bought."

I sit back in my chair, box in hand and just stare at him. Is this really my life? He bought me a new computer.

"So, P said she needed some new shoes, but not until it gets colder. We went ahead and got her a pair. I made sure they fit then went a half size bigger in case her feet grow between now and then. I remember Mom doing that with my little sister, Pepper."

"Easton," I breathe his name as tears prick the back of my eyes.

"And this," he ignores me, "this is for you. P and I thought that you would like something new that smelled good." He grins pointing to the bag from Bath & Body Works.

"I got this, Mommy," Paisley's sleepy voice greets us.

I place the computer and the bag on the table, expecting her to come to me; instead, she stops beside Easton and holds her arms up for him. He doesn't even hesitate to pick her up and place her on his hip. I watch as she rests her head on her shoulder and he rubs her back.

"You hungry, princess?" he asks.

"Did you eat all the cookies?" she asks.

"I would never," he says as if she offended him. "How about I whip us up some dinner while Mommy finishes her schoolwork. You any good at making spaghetti?"

"The bestest," she tells him. "But look," she turns to me, "we builded it at the Build-A-Bear." She holds out a big brown bear for me to see. "I gots to pick out her clothes too."

"That's all in this bag." Easton shows her the bag sitting on the table.

"That's great, P. Did you have a good time?" It's a stupid question by the smile tilting her lips. I can feel some of the earlier tension sliding away watching the two of them. An outsider looking in would never be able to tell that she's not his daughter. The love they have for one another is palpable.

"I did. But East said no cookie until after dinner." She pouts.

"You actually said no?" I manage to ask over the lump in my throat.

"Not really. More like suggested them for dessert and she agreed." He places P back on her feet. "Why don't you go put your bear in the living room? We don't want her to get dirty or worse, burnt while we're cooking."

"Okay." She skips off to the living room.

"Larissa," he says. I look up from where I've been staring at my lap. "You're my girls." He says it so simply, as if those three words don't make my heart feel as though it could jump out of my chest. "I want to take care of you. I can do it, so please let me. I loved my time with her today, seeing her face light up. I love knowing that buying you this computer is going to make your life easier. Let me do that."

A tear falls down my cheek. "T-thank you, Easton."

"My pleasure, baby." He kisses my forehead. "Now, I'm going to go make us dinner, with Princess Paisley as my assistant, while you set up your new laptop and finish whatever it is you need to do."

"Ready," Paisley says, bouncing into the room and grabbing his hand.

"Let's do this." He scoops her up in his arms and skips with her into the kitchen.

I take a minute to catch my breath, to get my emotions under control before opening the box and pulling out the laptop. It's nicer than any I've ever owned. Easton Monroe has changed my life. He supports me. He's there for me and for my daughter. I'm madly in love with him, and I just about blurted it out. I don't want to tell him I love him after he drops a chunk of cash on me and my daughter. I want it to be the right moment. Plus, there's a little bit of me that worries that it's too soon. That although I know he cares about me, he might not be where I am. I'll be keeping it to myself a little longer, just to be on the safe side.

CHAPTER 29
Easton

I LEAVE TODAY FOR A five-day stint on the road. While it's my job as a professional baseball player, it's the norm and what I do, this time I really don't want to go. Over the last couple of months since Larissa and Paisley have become permanent fixtures in my life, I've thought this before every road trip. This one though is different. It's killing me to know I'm not going to be here this week.

It's her birthday.

My princess turns five on Saturday, and I won't be here.

When you have a job like mine, you accept there are things you're going to miss. Anniversaries, birthdays, holidays... heck, some of the guys miss their kids being born. I knew this going into it, and with my parents and my sister, it sucked I missed those occasions with my family, but it never really reached me, the feeling that I was actually missing out, deep in my gut. Not like it is today.

I don't want to go.

I want to be here.

Larissa offered to hold off on Paisley's party, which is a few of her friends from the T-ball team coming over for games, as well as cake and ice cream. I told her not to do that. It's not fair to Paisley or Larissa. She already has it planned and the weekend off work.

I hate I can't be here, and have yet to break it to Paisley. I don't know how she's going to take the news, but I'm on my way to their place now to tell her. I'm also going to give her all the gifts that I bought her. I might have gone a little over the top because I knew I wasn't going to be able to be with her on her special day. Larissa is going to kill me when she sees exactly how over the top I've gone.

Pulling into the driveway, I climb out of my truck and grab the big box, and the two gift bags. I'll have to come back out to get the present that's in the back of the truck. Actually, I think I'll just let her unwrap it in the back.

"East!" Paisley throws open the front door and her eyes grow wide. "What are those?"

"Are you supposed to be answering the door on your own?" I ask her.

"No, she's not," Larissa says, catching up to her at the door.

"Princess, you know that's dangerous."

"I know, but I seed you in the window and I missed you so, so much." She bats her long eyelashes at me, and I want to fold, I do, but her safety is important.

Placing the bags and the box on the swing, I bend down to her level. "I understand that, and I missed you too. Do you know how much my heart would hurt if something happened to you? Do you know how much your mommy and I would miss you?"

Her eyes well up with tears. "I'm sorry." Her bottom lip quivers.

"Come here." I pull her into my arms and hug her tightly. "I'm not mad at you, Paisley, but I would be if something happened to you. Mommy and I would both be really sad if you were hurt or taken from us."

She nods and sniffs. "Are those for me?" she asks.

I bite my lip to keep from laughing. I know she's four, well almost five and doesn't understand the dangers, but I hope she will think twice before opening the door again without an adult with her. "They are," I tell her.

"Mommy, do you see dat?" She points to the swing.

"I do," Larissa says. "Why don't you go inside and we can bring them in."

"Okay, but hurry," she says, dashing off into the house.

"Really, Easton?" Larissa asks.

"What?" I play dumb.

"You're spoiling her."

"I know." I grin.

"What happens when she begins to expect this and I can't make it happen? I'm a single mom on one income."

"You also have a very rich boyfriend who loves to spoil both of you." I lean in for a kiss, but she turns her head giving me her cheek.

"It's too much. You just took her shopping and got her shoes and a bear, that she absolutely loves by the way."

"Good. I hope to do more of that. For both of you." I snake my arm around her waist and bring her into my embrace. "Look, I'm bummed I'm not going to be here on Saturday. I wanted to make up for it. I have to break the news to her that I can't be here and that's killing me. Besides, she's my princess," I say, kissing her neck.

"Fine," she grumbles. "But we need to talk about how you spoil her. You need to dial it down a bit, mister."

With one hand behind my back, I cross my fingers. "We do," I agree, not meaning it. Nothing she says will keep me from giving them the world, or at least stop me from trying to give it to them.

"Paisley," I yell, and she rushes to the door. Her nose is pushed up against the screen, and the smile on her face is infectious. "I was wondering if you know of anyone who's having a birthday soon?"

"Me, oh me." She jumps up and down.

"Come here." She wastes no time pushing open the screen door and barreling into me. "I need to tell you something."

"Okay," she says.

I take a seat on the steps, and she climbs into my lap. "I leave tomorrow for a whole week. Do you know what that means?"

"You have to play baseball. Are you sure that's work?" she asks.

I throw my head back and laugh. "Yeah, princess, it's work. They pay me to play."

"That's what I want to do when I grow up."

"You can be anything you want," I say, kissing the top of her head. "That also means I won't be able to be here on Saturday to celebrate your birthday." Her lip quivers and I rush to say more. "But I thought today we could pretend it was your birthday and that makes it super special because it's just the three of us, which means I get you both all to myself. It's like my present."

"But I miss you," she whispers.

"I know, sweet girl. I'll miss you too. Sometimes adults have to do things they don't want to. If I could stay home with you and your mom, I would, but this is my job and I have to go."

"Don't worry, East." She places her tiny hands on each of my cheeks. "Mommy can cord the game and I can see you. I'll still love you if you miss my party."

I kiss her nose and hug her tightly. "I love you, Paisley Gray. You are a special little girl."

She nods. "That's what Mommy says too."

I look up at Larissa, and she's shaking with silent laughter as unshed tears glimmer in her eyes. "Right, so I have some gifts for the birthday girl."

She wiggles in my lap, barely able to contain her excitement. "Can I open them?"

"You sure can. But you have to open the box first," I tell her, helping her off my lap. She rushes to the swing and tears into the box. Her shriek rings out causing me to wince. The neighbors are probably wondering what the hell is going on over here.

"East! I love her so, so much, and she looks just like me."

"She does. Do you want to know what her name is?" I ask. She nods. "Her name is Maisley." I wink.

"Just like the story!" She cheers and drags the box from the swing over to me. "Can you help me?"

"I can, but before we get her out, why don't you open the rest of your presents?" She rushes back to the swing and tears into the bags. Between the two bags, there are eight outfits, four for her and four for her American Girl doll so they can match. I went a little crazy.

"Mommy, look!" She holds up each outfit. "Me and Maisley can match.

"I see. Can you tell Easton, thank you?"

She drops the clothes on the porch and rushes to me. Her arms wrap around my neck and she squeezes with what I imagine is all her might. "Thank you so, so much, East. You're my bestest friend."

"You're welcome, princess. I have one more for you. You ready for it?"

"I don't see any more," she says, looking around.

"That's because it's still in my truck. Come here." I hoist her up in my arms and hold my hand out for Larissa. When we get to the back of my truck, Paisley's eyes grow wide.

"What is it?" she whispers.

"I don't know. You're going to have to unwrap it and find out." Pulling down the tailgate, I lift her into the back of the truck and tell her to have at it. I pull Larissa into me and wrap my arms around her.

"You went overboard," she says, resting her head and her hands on my chest.

"Nah, just wanted it to be special for her."

"A doll's house!" Paisley shrieks. "I wanted one so, so bad, oh thank you." She jumps up and down, causing the truck to shake.

"Careful, P," Larissa calls out. "How did you know?" she asks me.

"I didn't. I just remember seeing her room, and that she didn't have one. When I went to the store and asked for a good gift for a five-year-old girl, the clerk was helpful saying she always wanted a doll's house when she was that age, but they were too expensive. I had her show them to me, and once I saw it, I knew it was perfect."

"Thank you, Easton."

"Anything for my girls." I kiss her temple.

"All right, P, let's get your doll and clothes in the house." She turns to me. "You need help with this?"

"Nope, I got it. I'll be right in." After we get everything packed inside and the paper thrown away, Larissa and I curl up on the couch while Paisley plays with her doll's house in the corner of the living room. She insisted we leave it there. She was too excited to wait to make a spot for it in her room. It was the perfect day with my girls. One I hope we can repeat as often as possible.

CHAPTER 30
Larissa

I T TOOK ME OVER AN hour to convince Easton that I could drive to the stadium on my own. He wanted Paisley and me to ride with him. However, keeping my five-year-old daughter occupied for that length of time is a challenge at best. He eventually relented, as long as I promised to call him as soon as we got here. Which is what has me reaching for my phone as soon as we're parked.

"You here?" he answers.

"Yeah, we just pulled in."

"Okay, are you in the players' lot with the pass I gave you?"

"We are."

"Perfect, go to the side door. There will be a security guard there. I'm on my way to get you."

"You don't have to."

"Baby, I'm on my way," he says, ending the call.

"Was that East, Mommy?" Paisley asks.

"Sure was. He's going to meet us at the door."

Paisley cheers and unbuckles her booster seat. After gathering my purse, which holds a few toys for Miss P, and making sure I have my cell and my keys, I lock up my car and we head to the door. East is there waiting on us.

"There're my girls," he says, giving me a quick kiss, then lifting Paisley in his arms and kissing her on the cheek as well.

"You found us," Paisley says happily.

"Of course I did. You ready to watch me play?"

"Yes, and my other friends too. Did you tell them I was here?" she asks, speaking of the other players we've met.

"I didn't, but I will." She nods like she's happy with that answer. "I have your tickets," he tells me. "You're going to be sitting with Carol. She's Mark's wife. He's our pitcher. She's super nice and prefers to sit in the stands where the action is."

"Thank you. I'm sure we'll be fine."

"I'll walk you to where you need to be. Then I need to get back." He leans in and kisses my cheek. "You look good with my number on your back."

I blush. "East, it's fine. You don't want to deal with the fans. I can manage to find our seats on my own." I ignore his comment—not much we can do about it in a crowded stadium.

"You sure?" he asks, sliding his hand around the back of my neck and pulling me in for a kiss, causing Paisley, who is still in his arms, to giggle.

"Good luck today." I kiss him one more time. This time just a quick peck on the lips.

"Good luck," Paisley says, kissing his cheek.

"My girls are here; it's going to be a good game." He sets P back on her feet and guides us into the building. "This is where we part ways. Call me if you need anything."

"Oh, you mean while you're out on the field doing your job?" I ask him. "We're fine, East. Don't worry about us. Just go and have a good game. We'll be here when it's over."

"I love that," he says softly. "I love that the two of you are here and will be when the game is over."

"That's because we love you, silly," Paisley chimes in.

"I love you too, princess." He's said those very words to her before, but every time it causes my heart to tip over in my chest. I know he means it. I can see it in his eyes and hear it in his voice. He truly loves my daughter. Then again, maybe that's just me. Maybe more of my heart is wrapped up in him.

We find our seats easily enough, and as soon as we sit, the blonde in the chair next to Paisley turns in her seat. "You must be Larissa." She holds out her hand. "I'm Carol. It's nice to meet you."

"Yes, you as well."

"I'm Paisley." My daughter holds out her hand, and Carol laughs.

"I've heard all about you, Paisley. It's nice to meet you too."

"You know me?"

"Easton couldn't stop talking about you," she tells her.

"Oh, yeah, he loves me." She says it so nonchalantly you have to smile.

"You ready for the game?" Carol asks her.

"Yep. My East is gonna win," Paisley tells her.

"Sorry," I tell Carol. "She's quite taken with him."

"Is she the only one?" Carol smiles coyly. "Sorry, I'm overstepping, but I've known him for a while now, and he's quite smitten."

"He's not the only one," I admit, just as we're instructed to rise for the national anthem. Once the players are announced and the first pitch is thrown, Paisley bounces in her seat, cheering for Easton and the Blaze.

At the beginning of the seventh innings, my daughter turns to me with a serious expression on her face. "Mommy, can East be my daddy?"

I freeze at her question, not knowing how to answer her. Carol catches my eyes and gives me a warm smile, letting me know she heard her. "Sweetheart, it's not that simple."

"But he loves us, and that's what daddies do. They love you and your mommy."

My sweet girl. "That's true, but those kinds of things take time. Your biological daddy is in heaven, so that makes things not so easy."

"Sure it is. I'm gonna ask him."

I don't know what else to say, so I leave it alone. It's not until the bottom of the ninth, when East is standing just outside the dugout where we have a clear view, that I realize leaving it alone wasn't the best way to handle it. Not when Paisley stands up in her chair and screams his name. He turns to face us, a smile spread wide across his face. I'll give him credit, it doesn't falter when she screams, "Will you be my daddy?"

The crowd around us falls to a hush while my daughter stands on her chair, hands on her hips, waiting for his answer. He blows her a kiss because he's up to bat. I expect her to freak out, but she doesn't. She sits back down and looks over at me. "Told you he loved us," she says, then goes back to watching the game.

The crowd picks back up as if the scene never happened, and I breathe a sigh of relief, that is until the mean girls behind us start running their mouths.

"What kind of mother lets her kid think that Easton Monroe could be her father?"

"Pathetic."

"She needs to teach her about life."

On and on they spew hate.

"Like he would ever take them on," one of them sneers. "Like he wants a ready-made family. As if."

Paisley whips around and points her little finger. "My East says speak from your heart. Your heart is not very nice. He loves us. My Easton, me, and my mommy are a family," she tells them.

I was hoping she hadn't heard them. To prevent a bigger spectacle and cause problems for East, I gather our stuff, pick Paisley up, and we leave. We're only missing half of the last innings, and she doesn't need to hear this shit. I want to go off on them, but I'm trying to set an example for my daughter, and I don't want to embarrass East more than we already have. I'm sure he's going to regret asking us to the game.

Instead of sticking around, I send him a text.

> Hey, heading out early. You had a great game. Call me when you get home.

I get Paisley, who is crying big fat crocodile tears, in the car and calmed down before leaving the stadium. She falls asleep on the way home, which is a good thing. I need time to process what just happened. I carry P to her room, pulling off her shoes and shutting her bedroom door.

I'm too fired up to sit, so I find myself pacing back and forth. The more I think about what happened, the more upset I get. They can talk shit about me, but about my daughter with her sitting right there.... What kind of mother am I that I didn't go off on them? I didn't defend my baby. I think I was in shock that they would say those things knowing I could hear them. Paisley was so engrossed in the game, I assumed she didn't. That's what I get for assuming.

Hot tears prick my eyes. My cell rings, and I see his name flash on my screen. I can't answer. As soon as I hear his voice, I'll lose my barely-there grip on my emotions. Instead, I send him to voice mail. The anger swirls at the pain of seeing Paisley's tears and thinking of the way she defended him, defended us, and I did nothing.

Thirty minutes later, I'm still pacing and still mad at myself for just rushing out of there, but I didn't want to cause a scene. I go back and forth from it being the right answer to being a coward. I'm a mess.

When a strong knock sounds at the door, I know it's him. Sucking in a deep breath, I make my way to the door. As soon as I pull it open and I see him, I lose it, and the tears rush down my face.

CHAPTER 31
Easton

M Y FIST BOUNCES OFF HER door, loud enough I'm sure to cause concern from her neighbors. I couldn't give a fuck about them; all I care about are the two people who are my entire world, and the damn door is all that's keeping me from them.

I raise my fist to pound again, but the door swings open. Larissa is there, tears in her eyes. "Baby," I reach for her, but she steps out of my reach, and the tears begin to fall.

"Don't," she warns.

"Larissa, can we talk about this? Carol told me what happened. I'm just as upset as you are, but pushing me away is not the answer. Nothing they said matters. Nothing."

My phone rings. Glancing at the screen, I see it's my mother. I'm going to have to call her back. I slide my phone back in my pocket, ready to fight for her. It immediately rings again. Pulling it out again, I see it's my mom, and worry rushes over me. "I'm sorry, I know we're in the middle of a conversation, but it's my mother, and she never calls right back. I'm afraid something might be wrong."

"Answer it," she says, waving a hand in my direction. She wipes the corner of her eye, and my heart cracks seeing her tears. I never want to see her cry.

My phone stops then starts back up again; this time I answer. "Hey, Mom, is everything okay?"

"Fine, except for the fact that it's been weeks since I've talked to my son. By the way, good game."

"Thanks. I'm good," I assure her. "I talked to Dad a couple of weeks ago."

"That's your father," she scolds me.

"I know, I'm sorry. How are you and the rest of the Monroe clan?" I ask. She rambles on, but I'm not listening. All my attention is on the woman standing in front of me, wiping away her tears. I need to end this call with my mother, tell her that I'll call her back, but I also need this time to get my thoughts in order. I'm in for the fight of my life, to prove to her that she and Paisley are a part of me and I want them in my life for now and for always.

"East, are you even listening?"

"Sorry, what?" I ask, letting her draw me back into the conversation.

"Your dad said you met someone." Her voice is low, almost a whisper, as if it's a secret she's not supposed to know.

"Yeah, I met someone," I admit. Larissa's eyes snap to mine. They're still brimming with tears. "I met this woman. She's amazing, Mom. She's gorgeous and smart, busts her ass every day, and she has these bright green eyes that remind me of emeralds. She's a great mom, reminds me a lot of you." My eyes never leave Larissa's.

"She has kids?" Mom asks.

"Yeah, a little girl. Her name is Paisley, and I swear to you, she stole my heart the minute I met her." I watch Larissa as she bites down on her bottom lip.

Mom chuckles. "How's that going? Do you get along with her? How old is she?"

"She just turned five, and yeah, we get along great. She asked me if I would be her daddy," I confess as I watch a tear slide down Larissa's cheek.

Mom gasps. "How do you feel about that?"

"I want nothing more than to be her daddy. It may not be my blood running through her veins, but I couldn't love her more if it were."

"Oh, East," Mom gushes. "What about her mother?"

"I love her. I love them both." A sob breaks from Larissa's chest. "Listen, Mom, Larissa's here and we were in the middle of something. Can I call you back later?"

"She's there? East, you should have sent me to voice mail," she scolds.

"I tried," I tell her with a chuckle.

"Sorry," she replies sheepishly. "Call me later. Love you."

"Love you too, Mom." I end the call and slide my phone back in my pocket before holding my hand out for Larissa. She takes it and allows me to lead us to the couch. She sits, and I sit across from her on the coffee table, gripping her hands in mine. "I love you, Ris, and I love Paisley. That's all that matters to me. I don't care who says what or who thinks what about us. All that matters to me is the two of you. I want her smiles when she comes home from school, or when she catches a fly ball. I want to tuck her in at night and read her however many princess stories it takes for her to fall asleep."

"She loves you too," she says through her tears.

I nod, because I know she does. She's told me several times. "Then, I want to be able to climb into bed with you and talk about our day while I hold you in my arms. I want to make love to you until we're too exhausted and have no choice but to fall asleep." The tears are falling faster, but I push through, needing to bare my soul to her. "I know life with me won't be easy. I have five or six years left before I won't be able to play anymore. I know it's a lot to ask, but I need you to take a leap of faith. Trust that we can do that. That we can be a family. I want to be her daddy, and I want you to be my wife."

Her mouth drops open as I lower myself to my knees. "I wasn't sure when I was going to ask you, I wanted it to be perfect, and I need to talk to Paisley," I admit, and she smiles through her tears. "But I want to marry you. I want you both to have my last name, and I want to have more babies with you." I place my hand on her belly. "I know you worry, baby. But I need you to trust me. I won't hurt either of you. All I want to do is love you, and make Paisley feel every bit like the princess she is and make you my queen."

A laugh breaks free, and her smile is blinding. "I love you too," she says, scooting to the edge of the couch. "My heart cracks when I think about not being with you. When I think about telling Paisley that you're no longer going to be around. I just worry—"

I cut her off by pressing my lips to hers.

When the kiss ends, she admits, "She stood up for us, and I didn't. I was too afraid to cause a scene, so I grabbed her and our stuff and hightailed it out of there. What kind of mother does that? What kind of mom doesn't stick up for her kid?"

"Didn't you?" I ask her. "You showed her how to be the bigger person."

She laughs humorlessly. "That was you. She told them her East says to speak from your heart and that their hearts were not nice."

"That's my girl," I say, cupping her face in my hands. "I love you. You're an amazing mother who was put into a tough situation. I need you to know that no matter what, I'm on your side. God forbid something like that happens again, but if it does, my family comes first. You and Paisley are my family."

"I love you," she says, wiping her eyes.

"Say no more. That's all I needed to know. Trust in the love we have for one another. Trust me to take care of both of you." I kiss her one more time. "Now, I need to take our little girl out on a date, so she and I can have a chat." I stand and pull her with me. "You okay with me taking her out to dinner?"

She nods, more tears tracking down her cheeks. "Yeah. I'm okay with that. She's in her room."

"Love you, Ris." I kiss her one more time then head down the hall to get our daughter. The reality that I get to call her that, that I can tell her that she can call me Daddy is humbling and exciting. It beats any win I've ever had in baseball.

Paisley's awake when I enter her room. She holds her arms open for me, and I scoop her up in my arms, giving her a big hug. "Those girls said bad things," she tells me.

"I know they did, princess. I'm sorry."

"S'okay."

"Hey, I thought that you and I could go out to dinner. Just the two of us."

"Really?" she asks, perking right up.

"Yeah, your mom said it was okay."

"Is Mommy not gonna go too?"

"Nope, this is just us. We can go have pizza and bring her leftovers."

"Cheese pizza?"

"Is there any other kind?"

"Yay!" She jumps off the bed, grabs my hand, and pulls me down the hall. "Mommy, are you sad 'cause we gonna get pizza?"

"No, sweetie. You have fun with East and be good, okay?"

"Okay, Mommy. Come on, East." Still holding my hand, she tries to pull me to the door.

Sliding my other hand behind Larissa's neck, I kiss her slowly. "We'll be back soon."

On the way to get pizza, Paisley talks about the game, how fun it was and how mad she was at the "mean girls" when they said I wouldn't be her daddy.

We settle in a booth, Paisley sitting across from me because "that's what big girls do." We order our food, and once our drinks are delivered, it's go time.

"Princess, you asked me a pretty important question today."

"I did?" I have to fight back my grin at her confusion.

"You did. You asked me if I would be your daddy. Do you know what that means?"

"It means that you love me and kiss Mommy and tuck me in at night."

"That's right. I want to be your daddy more than anything. I also want to make your mommy my wife. I want to ask her to marry me."

"What does that mean?"

"Well, Mommy would change her last name to Monroe."

"I want my last name to be Monroe."

"I would love that." This little girl is my light.

"So are you marrying me too?"

I smile at this kid. Reaching into my pocket, I pull the tiny charm bracelet out. I picked it up along with the ring for Larissa before the game today. I found myself in the jewelry store earlier this week, and both items just felt right. I've never been more relieved of my decision than in this moment. This is the right time. It might be soon, but love is love.

"Oh, that's pretty," she says, following my hands.

"When I marry your mommy, I'll give her a ring. This is for you. It's a charm bracelet. Here is a baseball and a bat, and here is half a heart."

"Why only half?"

"Because your mommy has the other half. I love both of you very much, and I would be honored to be your daddy and to give you my last name." Reaching across the table, I put the bracelet on her tiny wrist. "Paisley Gray, do I have your permission to marry your mommy?"

"And me too," she says, bouncing on her seat.

Her declaration has me smiling and choking up with tears. "Yeah, princess, and you too." We finish our pizza and pack the leftovers up in a box for Larissa. All the way home, she talks about anything and everything, filling the silent truck with chatter. It's something I never knew I was missing.

"Hey," Larissa says, meeting us at the door.

"Mommy, look." Paisley holds her wrist out. "East is gonna marry us, and we're gonna change our names." She looks up at me. "What is it again?"

"Monroe," I tell her.

"That's it." She nods. "I'm gonna be Paisley Gray Monroe, and you're gonna be Mommy Monroe," she says as serious as can be.

"That's right, princess. Why don't you go take a seat on the couch? Mommy and I will be right there." She skips off into the other room without objection.

"Sounds like that went well." She's looking up at me with a hint of a smile on her face. Almost as if she's afraid to hope that what her daughter just told her is true.

"It did." I take her hands in mine and drop to one knee. "I love you, Ris. The moment I met you, I knew you were different. I just didn't realize how meeting you would change my life. I didn't know that not only you, but that little girl in there, would wind your way around my heart so much so that it's no longer mine. Take a leap of faith with me, baby." Reaching into my pocket, I pull out the little black box that holds the ring I picked out for her. "Larissa, will you do me the incredible honor of becoming my wife?"

Tears stream down her cheeks, but her blinding smile tells me these are the good kind of tears, the kind that let you know the impact of the moment. "Yes," she says, placing her hand over her mouth.

Standing, I slide the ring on her finger and pull her in for a kiss. Being here with her in my arms, I realize that happiness lies in those you love and the love they give back to you. Me and my girls, we've got that in spades.

15 MONTHS LATER
Easton

IT TOOK ME TWO MONTHS from the day I proposed to convince Larissa to give up her apartment and move in with me.

Paisley was on board from day one; of course it helped that I had one of the spare bedrooms turned into a princess room for her. With Princess P on my team, we wore her down.

It took me another four months to get her to set a date and another six after that for her to become my wife. Every day with the two of them is better than the last. There's laughter that fills what used to be the silent rooms of my house; it's now a home. A home with my girls.

Today is a special day in so many ways. It's our three-month wedding anniversary, and you can bet your ass I'm celebrating. Every fucking day is a celebration with the two of them in my life. It's also the anniversary of the day my adoption went through, when *I* became a Monroe. Not a day goes by that I'm not grateful for all that my father has brought into our lives. He's the man I want to be, hope to be for my wife and my daughter. Did I mention that as of today, I'm also officially a father?

Today my princess officially became a Monroe. We signed the papers at the courthouse this morning and then went out to breakfast to celebrate. It was already a special day, the day I gained my father. The man who has always been there for me. Now, I get to be that man. I get to show him what he taught me. How to be a man, how to love. How to fight for those you love. He taught me how to be a father. Not that anything has changed because of a signed piece of paper. Paisley started calling me Daddy the day I proposed to them, and never looked back. In my heart, she's mine. I don't need a piece of paper to prove that.

My daughter.

"So, Miss Monroe," I say to my daughter. "What would you say if I told you we're going to take a trip today?" I ask as she forks in another bite of her Mickey Mouse pancakes.

Her eyes light up with excitement. "Where?" she asks with her mouth full, causing me to laugh and my wife to cringe.

"Atlanta."

"Really?" she asks, dropping her fork.

"Really."

"Yay!" she cheers, gaining us the attention of those sitting around us. She wiggles around in her chair almost tipping over; luckily her grandma is there to catch her.

"Easy there," my mother-in-law, Helen, says, grabbing the chair and steadying her.

"You coming with us?" Paisley asks her.

"She is," I say, knowing she's not convinced going is the best. I've been hounding her for two weeks now, and she keeps saying she doesn't want to intrude. She's family, and we need her to be there.

"When do we leave?" Paisley asks, setting her glass of milk back on the table. She has a line across her top lip and looks like one of those Got Milk commercials.

"After breakfast, so you need to finish up," Larissa tells her.

With a nod, she dives back into her breakfast with gusto, making us all laugh.

The flight to Atlanta is a short one. Dad is waiting for us at the airport, and as soon as Paisley sees him, she runs into his arms. "Grandpa," she says excitedly.

I watch as my father picks her up and settles her on his hip. She's getting too big for that, but he doesn't see her as often as he and my mom would like. "Hey, Princess P," he says, kissing her cheek.

"Did you know that today I'm a Monroe?" she asks him.

His misty eyes cause me to swallow back my own emotions. "I did, sweet girl," he says, hugging her close.

"Hey, Dad," I say, clapping him on the shoulder.

"East. Hey, Larissa, Helen, glad you could join us," he greets them.

After the hellos, we head to his waiting SUV. Paisley fills the car with chatter about our day and the events at the courthouse. She then goes on to tell us that it's "the bestest day ever" since all her family is together. Little does she know that we really are all going to be together. It just didn't feel right having this moment without the entire Monroe clan. One phone call to my mom, grandma, and Aunt Carrie, and the wheels were set in motion.

Arriving at the farm, memories from my childhood assault me. This place is like home. I'm thrilled to be sharing it with my wife and daughter. Reaching for Paisley and lifting her out of the SUV, she holds my hand as we walk inside. The house is quiet, but I know where they are. As we turn the corner in the living room, everyone yells "Surprise!" causing P to squeal.

"Look, Daddy." She points to the banner that says, Paisley Gray Monroe in bright pink letters. That's it, just her name. Not welcome home or welcome to the family, as she's already so ingrained in our lives that would be foolish. Instead, it's her new name, my last name that's now tacked on to the end of hers that adorns the sign.

I set her on her feet, and she makes her way around the room, getting hugs and kisses from her official aunts, uncles, and cousins. She's lapping up the attention like I knew she would. I knew coming home is what I needed today, what we all needed.

"Proud of you," my dad says from beside me.

"Who would have thought all those years ago, I'd become a father for the first time the same day that you did?"

He smiles at me and nods. "Love you, son."

"Love you too, Dad."

"What are my boys doing over here?" Mom asks, stepping into me and wrapping her arms around my waist.

"Just taking it all in," I tell her. She smiles up at me, giving my waist another squeeze. "Well, excuse me, but my granddaughter has a gift to open."

"Mom," I scold her.

"She's our princess, after all." She grins over her shoulder as she picks up a bag I missed and then takes a seat on the floor next to my daughter.

Larissa appears beside me, and I pull her into my arms. "Thank you," she whispers, not taking her eyes off our daughter.

"For what?"

"For loving us."

I laugh. "Baby, loving you is the easy part. It was getting you to love me back I had the issue with. I should be the one thanking you." She swats my chest playfully. We watch as Paisley opens her gift. It's a bracelet of some sort, and I'm just about to ask when Dad explains.

"It has her name on it."

"Paisley Gray Monroe," my daughter reads the words aloud. "Thank you, Grandma." She launches herself at my mother, and I can see the tears in her eyes from where I'm standing. Mom catches my eyes from across the room and smiles. I know what that smile means. Paisley is me, and my mom is Larissa. She knows what it meant to us and in turn how much it means to my girls.

Larissa turns in my arms and looks up at me. Her smile is blinding as unshed tears fill her eyes. She laughs softly as she wipes away an errant tear. "You got a minute?" she asks me.

"For you, I have a lifetime." Lacing my fingers with hers, I allow her to pull me out on the back deck. "I used to worry," she says once the door is shut behind us and she's back in my arms, her back to my front as we look out over the landscape. "I used to constantly worry and never felt settled. That changed when I met you."

I kiss the top of her head. I've seen the change in her; it's nothing she has to tell me.

"I think he brought you to us. He knew that it would take an amazing man, one full of love and patience and understanding to break through my walls. I like to believe that he picked you for us. That he knew you would be the father she needed, the partner I needed."

"I like the sound of that." It's hard to think about everything she lost and my heart aches for her, but then we wouldn't be where we are today. I like to think that everything happens for a reason. We might not know what those reasons are at the time, but we have to have faith that everything works out as it should.

"The last time I had this conversation, the day started out great and ended not so much. This time, I can feel it in my gut that it's different. I'm not worried."

"Babe, you've lost me," I tell her. I have no clue what she's talking about.

She turns in my arms and presses a kiss to the corner of my mouth. "I have a secret," she whispers.

"I'm your husband. We don't have secrets."

"This time we do." She grins.

"Larissa," I warn. I hate not being involved in every aspect of their lives. I never want to miss a minute. It's hard enough being away from them during the season.

Grabbing her phone out of her back pocket, she taps the screen a few times, then turns it to face me. "I got you something," she says softly.

My eyes focus on the screen, and it takes me a minute to realize what I'm looking at. "Is that?"

"You're going to be a daddy, again," she adds.

My hands grip her hips, pulling her impossibly close. "We're pregnant?"

"We are. We're in the first trimester."

"I don't know what that means? Are you okay? Is the baby okay? Have you been sick? Why didn't you tell me?" I fire off questions faster than she can answer them. Something that happens a lot between the two of us.

"It means I'm about seven weeks, just under two months along. I've not been sick, a little nauseous, but nothing otherwise. I was waiting for the right time to tell you. When we got our court date, I decided to wait. I wanted you to be here with your family when you found out."

"You're my family." I place my hand on her belly. "All three of you. We're having a baby," I say, pressing my lips to hers. "I love you, Larissa Monroe."

"I love you too, Easton Monroe."

I hear the door open behind us, and then my daughter says, "They do this all the time," causing everyone to laugh.

"Come here, princess," I say, and she doesn't hesitate to rush toward me. I step away from Larissa just in time to catch her in my arms. I reach for Larissa's hand, and we walk back inside. "Can I have your attention," I say to the room. It's packed full of family all here for us. "We have one more surprise for P, all of you, really," I admit.

Mom gasps and covers her mouth with her hands. Dad puts his arm around her, pulling her close. My eyes dance around the room, watching my little sister, my aunts and uncles, my grandparents, and cousins, all of them smiling as if they know our secret. I turn to Larissa. "Did you tell them?" I whisper.

She shakes her head, too choked up with emotion to speak.

"Paisley," I focus on my daughter, "today is a really special day," I tell her.

"I know. You and me are Monroes on the same day."

"That's right, we are. You know what else?"

"What?" Her eyes are wide with excitement.

"You're going to be a big sister." The room is silent, unbelievably so, as we all wait for her reaction. She looks at me then to her mother then back to me. "You better not be joking," she warns us.

"It's true," Larissa says, finding her voice.

"Yes!" She throws her arms in the air and cheers.

The room breaks out in celebration, and we receive hugs and well wishes. Paisley is so excited she talks about all the things she's going to do with her new baby brother or sister, including teaching them baseball. That has us all smiling. She runs off to play, and Larissa gets swept away by my aunts asking how she's feeling. That leaves me to sit back and soak up the moment. Life and family are what you make it. You love with all that you have, and live each day like it could be your last. That's exactly what I intend to do with my wife and children. Live each day with them as if it could be my last. I want to cherish their smiles and the sound of their laughter. My dad sweeps Paisley into his arms and sits her on his lap. Mom joins them, and they give her their full attention as her hands are flying this way and that, telling them a story. It's hard to figure out what she's saying; my girl has a vivid imagination.

Mom smiles over at me, and it's the same look she gave me earlier. The one that says she's proud of me and the man I've become. The one that tells me that to this day, I'm not the only one grateful that Jeff Monroe came into our lives. For so many years it was just us, quite the same way as Larissa and Paisley. Never again will they be alone. They'll be swarmed with love because that's what you do when you're a Monroe. You rally around those you love.

Paisley stands from my dad's lap and walks toward me. I bend down to greet her. "What's up, princess?"

"I knew this was going to be the best trip ever."

"Oh yeah? Why's that?"

"Because, Daddy," she says like I should know the answer.

"Because why, P?" I counter, tickling her side.

"Because you're my daddy and my Easton," she says, bringing me to my knees.

8 MONTHS LATER
Larissa

M Y HUSBAND IS DRIVING ME crazy. Exactly three weeks ago today, we brought our baby girl, Parker Elizabeth, home from the hospital. Easton has been amazing, fussing over all three of us, not letting me lift a finger. The first week or so, that was appreciated more than he could ever know, but today, today his hovering is driving me mad. It's the offseason, which means the four of us have been holed up in the house. Paisley is loving all her attention from Daddy... Mommy, not so much. I love my husband with all my heart, but he has to let me move, give me room to breathe.

As I finish feeding Parker, I stand to take her upstairs to change her diaper. "Sit, babe, I've got her." He holds his arms out, but I don't release my hold on our newborn baby girl.

"Easton, I'm perfectly capable of changing her diaper."

"I know, but you fed her." He points to my breasts and his eyes heat. Ignoring the way that one look from him makes me feel, makes me want things it's too soon to want, I focus on the issue at hand.

"I know that. But I can do this. I want to do this."

"Ris," he sighs.

"Why don't you call Drew and see if he wants to go to the cages?" I suggest.

"What?" he asks, appalled. "I can't leave you here alone." As if I'm not capable of caring for myself or our children.

"I won't be alone. Chloe is coming over to hang out with me. I haven't seen her since the first week we were home."

"I'll take the girls downstairs so you two can catch up."

"East." I say his name in my mom voice that always stops P in her tracks. "Go. Call the guys. Get out of the house. You need a break."

He scoffs. "I don't need a break from my family."

"Fine. We need a break from you."

His head jerks back and hurt flashes across his face. "Look. I love you. You are the most amazing father and husband. I love our life, but, babe, your hovering is driving me crazy. I've been down this road, and I traveled it mostly alone."

"But not this time. I promised you wouldn't ever do it alone again. I meant that."

"You're here for us every day. You've barely seen the guys since I told you we were pregnant. You need to still have a life, even though we have a family. It's a balance. You need this, trust me."

"What happens if you need me?"

"I'll call you. Chloe will be here. Nothing is going to happen. Go have a few beers, swing the bat a few or a hundred times. Go do manly things." I offer him a smile.

"Mommy, girls can hit balls too." Paisley's ever-present ears pick up on everything.

"That's right, princess," Easton agrees with her.

I move to stand in front of him. "I love you, Easton Monroe. You need a break, too. Go call Drew." Before he can protest again, the doorbell rings. "That's Chloe. We're going to catch up. You should do the same." With my index finger, I motion for him to come closer. He does as I ask and leans down so we are eye-to-eye. "I love you, slugger." I kiss him, taking my time. When I pull away, I see the worry leave him.

"Okay. But I'm not staying out long."

"Take all the time you need," I say, walking past him to let Chloe in.

"Aunt Chloe." Paisley runs and wraps her arms around Chloe's waist.

"Hey, P, you been helping Mommy and Daddy take care of your new baby sister?"

"When Daddy lets me." She giggles.

"I get it," Easton says, joining us at the front door. He has on a clean T-shirt, and his keys and phone are in his hand. "I can't believe I'm getting kicked out of my own home," he grumbles.

"Drew's waiting for your call." Chloe grins. She and Drew dated sporadically in the beginning, but these last few months, it seems to have become more serious.

"Love you." Easton bends to kiss the top of Paisley's head. He then gently presses a kiss to the top of Parker's who is asleep in my arms. "Love you, too," he says softly. His hand slides around the back of my neck as he leans in and kisses me. "Love you, wife. I'll be back soon." Standing, he points at Chloe. "You take care of them." The two of us throw our heads back in laughter.

"Go," I say, pushing on his back with my free hand.

"Love you," he calls over his shoulder, walking out the door.

"Gimme." Chloe holds her hands out for Parker. I transfer her over, then reach for Paisley's hand.

"Let's go sit on the couch." P is thrilled that she has my attention and leads the way. "So how are things with Drew?" I ask Chloe.

"Good. We've gotten closer these last few months."

"Exclusively?"

She smiles. "Not officially, but yeah, we're headed that way I think."

"You need one of those," I say, pointing to a sleeping Parker.

"I think you're right," she agrees, shocking the hell out of me.

"That's a first."

She shrugs. "Finding a guy who you know is going to stick around changes a girl's perspective."

"Don't I know it."

"Daddy never leaves," Paisley says, adding her two cents to the conversation, causing us to laugh.

"Your daddy just loves us and wants to take care of us."

"I know." She sighs. "Can I go play in my room?"

"Sure you can." Like lightning, she's off the couch and dashing upstairs to her princess room. Easton went all out when he asked us to move in with him. He took the liberty of making a pink and purple princess oasis for Paisley, the minute she saw it, she begged to move in. That was two months after he proposed. Since that day, the day of the proposal, our lives have been a whirlwind. A happy, full of love and laughter spiral of moments that I never want to forget.

Over the next couple of hours, Chloe and I catch up. She started a teaching job in the fall and loves it. I too finished my degree, but I'm not in any rush to find a job. Easton and I have talked about it, and I want to be home for the girls, at least for a little while. Something I didn't have the option to do when Paisley was little.

"It was good to catch up," Chloe says as we walk to the front door.

"Definitely. We need to not go so long next time."

"You have your hands full, with three kids." She winks, making me laugh.

"How about you and Drew come over this weekend for a barbecue?"

"You sure you feel up to it?"

"Yes, I need more best friend time. Besides, East won't let me lift a finger." I shrug.

"Spoiled." She grins. "And to think you almost let him go."

"Turns out he's the best thing that's ever happened to me."

"Aside from me of course," she jokes.

"And that. So I'll see you guys Saturday, say six o'clock?"

"We'll be here." We hug and then she's gone.

Paisley is still playing in her room. I can hear her singing along to her Disney movie. Parker is lights out, but I know she's going to be up soon; it's almost time for her to eat again.

I decide to sit down and read for a few minutes. As soon as I get my e-reader open and my feet propped up on the table, Parker's "I'm hungry" cry comes through the monitor.

"I'll get her," East says, scaring me.

"Hey, I didn't know you were back."

"I was trying to be quiet in case you girls were sleeping. You want to feed her down here or upstairs?"

"The nursery. I'm ready for bed."

"Me too. I'll get you two settled and then start P's bath." With a gentle hand, he pulls me from the couch and places his hand on the small of my back as we walk up the stairs to our daughters.

Forty minutes later, both kids are in their beds as we climb into ours. Easton aligns his body with mine, wrapping his arms around me. "I'm sorry for today." I remember the look of hurt that flashed across his face.

"No need for apologies. I needed to be told to back off a little."

"I love you, you know that, right?"

"I do. I love you, too, all three of you. The season starts in a few weeks, and I'm going to miss this. I'm trying to get as much time with the three of you as I can before I leave. However, it was nice to get out and hit up the cages for a couple of hours."

"I'm glad you got that time with the guys. Oh, I invited Chloe and Drew over on Saturday night for a barbecue."

"I take it I'll be braving the cold to man the grill?"

"As if you would let me." I laugh.

"I'd give you the world, Larissa Monroe."

"You already have."

3 YEARS LATER
Easton

I T'S AMAZING HOW THE LOVE of a good woman can change you. Change your perspective on life. Nothing mattered to me but baseball, until I found Larissa. I'm not sure how it happened, but I was the lucky bastard she decided to spend her life with. She gave me my daughters, all three of them.

Peyton coos in my arms while her mom sleeps peacefully. At just a few hours old, she's already captured my heart like the rest of my girls.

Larissa woke me up at a little after midnight when her water broke. I had just got to bed after being gone for an away game. I thank my lucky stars I was able to be here. The league now offers paternity leave, which I'm taking full advantage of. I was torn not wanting to let my team down, but at the end of the day, my girls are my home team, and this is where I need to be. I know any of the guys who were in my position, and those who have been, have made the same choice.

At just a few hours old, baby Peyton already has a firm grip on my finger. I can't help but wonder if she'll be into softball like her big sister Paisley? Parker is Paisley's shadow, I can't imagine that Peyton will be any different.

"Hey," my wife's sleepy voice greets me.

"Hey, beautiful," I whisper.

"How is she?"

"She's perfect, Ris. Just like her momma and her sisters. She's perfect," I say again, unable to take my eyes off our daughter.

"You're going to spoil her." My wife laughs.

"Of course I am." This time I pull my eyes away from my sleeping baby girl to look at Larissa. "Have you not figured it out yet? Spoiling my girls, all four of you is my life's mission." Her soft laughter meets my ears, and I cherish the sound. I vowed years ago to do whatever it took to keep the laughter on her lips. I'd like to think I've achieved that and continue to do so.

"I'm glad it worked out that your parents happened to arrive yesterday instead of today."

"It was nice to not have to drag the girls out of bed to get you here."

"Have you talked to them?"

"I texted Dad. He and Mom are going to bring them over after breakfast." I glance outside and see that the sun is just starting to rise. "Your mom went home to get some rest. She'll be back later."

Peyton fusses in my arms. "Are you hungry, sweet girl?" Her soft whimper is my answer. Carefully, I stand from the chair and help Larissa get adjusted. She lowers her gown, baring her full breast. "God, you're gorgeous." She blushes. After all this time, I can still make her blush.

"You've caught me, East. You can stop with the flattery." She shakes her head, but a soft smile plays on her lips.

"Never." I lean over and press my lips to hers. "You've never looked more beautiful than you do right this minute."

"You said that the day we were married, you said that when Parker was born, and a million other times."

"That's because you're more beautiful every damn day." Another quick kiss to the corner of her mouth and I place Peyton in her arms. Larissa coos at her for a few moments until Peyton decides she's had enough and wants to eat. Before Larissa has the chance to, as gently as I can, I guide her bare breast to Peyton, placing the nipple against her lips. She latches on immediately. I can't take my eyes off them. To see my wife feeding our daughter in the most natural form.... My heart is so full it feels as if it could burst from the love pumping through my veins.

When she's finished eating, I change Peyton's diaper and am just placing her back in Larissa's arms when the hospital room door pushes open. I hear Paisley first.

"Shh, Park, Mommy might be sleeping."

"I see baby sister," Parker replies.

"Hey, you," I open my arms, and both my girls know the drill. They come rushing as I capture them both in a hug. "You ready to meet your little sister?" They both nod. Standing to my full height, I pick Parker up, placing her on my hip and hold Paisley's hand. "Paisley and Parker, meet your sister Peyton," I introduce them just as I did Paisley to Parker when she was born.

"She's so tiny." Paisley is now ten and older beyond her years.

"Tiny," Parker agrees.

"Why don't you climb up here and you can hold her?" Larissa offers. Paisley wastes no time sliding in bed beside her mom.

"Me hold her," Parker says.

"You too," I agree. Paisley moves over, and I sit Parker in between her and Larissa. Taking Peyton from Larissa, I place her in Paisley's arms. I've placed Peyton just right so her legs are resting on Parker's lap, so she too feels as though she's getting to hold her little sister. "Hold her head," I instruct.

"I've got this," Paisley assures me.

"Got this," Parker agrees.

"Hey, son." Dad pulls me into a hug. "She's a beauty."

"Thanks." He releases me, and Mom takes his place. "Hey, Mom."

"You have a beautiful family, East."

Turning my head, I look over at my girls. The four of them are my everything. I can't imagine what my life would be like without them. "That I do," I agree with her. "That I do."

The rest of the day we have a revolving door of visitors. My mother-in-law came bearing food, of which we were both extremely grateful. Drew and Chloe stopped by but couldn't stay long. Chloe's mom was watching their three-month-old daughter, Clara. Fisher and Carr both stopped by with their wives, and the team sent a huge bouquet of flowers. It was a perfect day to celebrate the birth of our new baby girl.

11 YEARS LATER
Paisley

AS I STAND ON THE mound, I take a minute to memorize this moment. The crowd is loud, a sea of orange letting us know Tennessee fans are here in droves to support us. I know that in that sea of orange is my family. Mom, Dad, Parker, and Peyton. Grandma and Grandpa Monroe, Gram, Aunt Chloe, Uncle Drew, Clara, and Clayton, are all here to watch me and support my team.

My team that I've led to the Women's College Softball World Series. This is the last game in the series, and we're up by two. We only need one more out to end this game and win the series. This is the final innings of the game, and the final innings of my college career. I graduate next week with my bachelor's degree in sports medicine. I fell in love with the game around the same time Mom and Dad met. But it's not his shoes I followed in, it was Grandpa Monroe's. He too was a pitcher.

"Let's go, Monroe!" I hear from the crowd and know without a doubt that's my dad. He retired from the game my senior year of high school, and since then, there's not been one game he's missed. He does the same for my sisters. He's made it his life's goal to never miss another important event in our lives.

Taking a deep breath, I wind up the pitch and let it fly. Strike one. I wipe my sweaty palms on my pants and repeat the process two more times. As soon as the third strike is called, I drop to my knees. I don't even try to keep the tears from falling. My smile is wide as my team rushes me and we fall into a pile on the field. We did it. We won the Women's College World Series.

The next hour is filled with families swarming the field, along with reporters and photographers. It's a bitter-sweet moment, one I'll never forget. When two strong arms wrap around me and swirl me around in the air, I know immediately it's my dad.

"So damn proud of you, princess," he whispers just for me.

This man, my father has been here for me from day one. I don't know that I'll ever be able to show him what his love, his acceptance of me as his own has done for me.

When he finally places my feet on the ground, I turn to face him. "I love you, Daddy." I might be twenty-one, but he will always be my daddy and I will always be his princess. Nothing will ever change that. I see his eyes shimmer and he smiles.

"It's like I blinked and now you're this beautiful young woman, bringing her old man to his knees, just like you did when you were a little girl."

"You know, just speaking from the heart." I wink, making him laugh.

"Come here, you." He tugs me into a tight hug and gets invaded by Mom and my sisters.

"So what's next?" Parker, who is now fourteen asks.

"You gonna miss it?" Peyton adds.

I look over at my parents, who are wearing matching grins. "I'm taking life beyond the bases." Dad throws his head back and laughs, as does my mom. My sisters just grin. Those three words mean just as much to my family as "I love you." It's something Dad told Mom when they were dating and it's stuck with her, with us.

BONUS SCENE
The Wedding

S IX MONTHS IS TOO DAMN long to wait to marry the love of your life. But when that love is Larissa, you wait to give her the perfect wedding. You wait, giving her the time she needs so she knows that no matter what, you'll be there. My girls are stuck with me.

I'm standing at the altar watching, waiting for my girls. Larissa and I decided that she and Paisley would walk hand-in-hand down the aisle together. I'm not just pledging my love to Larissa today, but my daughter as well. Pride washes over me. She's been calling me Daddy for a while now, but soon it's going to be official. First thing Monday morning, before we leave for our honeymoon, we're signing the papers to begin the adoption process.

When the music starts to play, I turn and focus my gaze on the aisle. When I see my two beauties appear in white, I have to bite down on my tongue to keep a sob from escaping my lips. Somehow, from the moment I met her, I knew this was where we would end up. This is where I hoped we would end up.

As they get closer, Paisley bounces on her feet at her mom's side and calls out for me. "Daddy!" she says loudly. "Look at my dress." She pulls on some of the white lace to show me. The guests laugh. "It's so, so pretty," she says, oblivious to the fact that her mom is shushing her.

"You're beautiful," I say when they reach me. Bending down, I scoop her up in my arms and place her on my hip. "And you," I lean in and kiss Larissa's cheek, "you take my breath away." Her eyes shimmer with tears.

"Dearly beloved," the minister begins the service. I hold Paisley close, while holding Larissa's hand. "Easton," he gives me my cue.

Crouching down, I place P on her feet and take both her hands in mine. "Paisley, I know you have a daddy in heaven, and I'm honored you've chosen me to be your daddy here on earth. You are a bright, beautiful, vibrant little girl, and you have brought so much love and joy to my life." I have to stop to get my emotions in check. P is smiling with tears in her eyes as well. "Today, I pledge my love to you as your father. I'll be there for the good times and bad, to scare the boys away until your thirty." This gets a laugh from the crowd.

"To play catch with me?" she asks shyly.

"Yeah, princess, to play catch with you. I promise to love you, my daughter, all the days of my life."

She launches her little body at me, wrapping her arms around my neck. "I love you so, so much," she whispers.

"I love you, too, P." Standing with her still in my arms, I reach out for Larissa with my free hand.

"I do. For as long as I live, I do," she blurts. "You love us, unconditionally. I don't know what I did to deserve you, Easton Monroe, but I thank God every day for bringing you into our lives. I do," she says again.

"Easton?" the minister asks.

"I do," I say past the lump of emotion lodged in the back of my throat.

"A little out of order, but the same result," the minister chuckles. "By the power vested in me by the state of Tennessee, I now pronounce you, husband and wife. You may kiss your bride."

Snaking my free arm around her waist, I pull Larissa in and kiss her at the same time Paisley lifts her head from my shoulder and kisses my cheek.

Closing my eyes, I hold my entire world in my arms. I want to memorize this moment, this feeling of being complete. This feeling of knowing that as of today, not just in my heart but in the eyes of the law, we're a family.

Me and my girls.

I cannot thank you enough for taking the time to read
Beyond the Bases.
Paisley's story is next in **Beyond the Game.**

Other titles in the **Out of Reach Series:**

Beyond the Game – Book 2

Beyond the Play – Book 3

Beyond the Team – Book 4

Never miss a new release:
Newsletter Sign-up

Be the first to hear about free content, new releases, cover
reveals, sales, and more. kayleeryan.com/subscribe/

Discover more about Kaylee's books
kayleeryan.com/all-books/

CONTACT
Kaylee Ryan

Facebook:

bit.ly/2C5DgdF

Reader Group:

bit.ly/2OoyWDx

Goodreads:

bit.ly/2HodJvx

BookBub:

bit.ly/2KulVvH

Website:

kayleeryan.com/

ALSO BY
Kaylee Ryan

With You Series:
Anywhere with You | More with You | Everything with You

Soul Serenade Series:
Emphatic | Assured | Definite | Insistent

Southern Heart Series:
Southern Pleasure | Southern Desire
Southern Attraction | Southern Devotion

Unexpected Arrivals Series
Unexpected Reality |Unexpected Fight | Unexpected Fall
Unexpected Bond | Unexpected Odds

Riggins Brothers Series:
Play by Play | Layer by Layer | Piece by Piece
Kiss by Kiss | Touch by Touch | Beat by Beat

Entangled Hearts Duet:
Agony | Bliss

Cocky Hero Club:
Lucky Bastard

ALSO BY
Kaylee Ryan

Mason Creek Series:
Perfect Embrace

Standalone Titles:
Tempting Tatum | Unwrapping Tatum | Levitate
Just Say When | I Just Want You | Reminding Avery

Hey, Whiskey | Pull You Through | Remedy
The Difference | Trust the Push | Forever After All
Misconception | Never with Me

Out of Reach Series:
Beyond the Bases | Beyond the Game
Beyond the Play | Beyond the Team

Co-written with Lacey Black:

Fair Lakes Series:
It's Not Over | Just Getting Started | Can't Fight It

Standalone Titles:
Boy Trouble | Home to You | Beneath the Fallen Stars

Co-writing as Rebel Shaw with Lacey Black:
Royal | Crying Shame

ACKNOWLEDGMENTS

Some of you already know this, other may not. Beyond the Bases started out at a novella for a Kindle World. When the program was terminated, I had a novella that needed tweaked to take out the world tie-ins and add some words to be ready to publish. I loved the story and felt like I could expand on it, give more depth so that's what I did. I hope you fell in love with Easton, Larissa and Paisley. They were a joy to write, especially Paisley.

To my team:

Sommer Stein, Perfect Pear Creative Covers, I don't know how you do it. I give you an image, the basic plot points and every time you produce a cover that not only captures the book, but draws you to it. Thank you for your design genius and all that you do.

Sara Eirew produced another amazing image. I've been holding onto this one for a while now and I'm glad I finally had the book to fit it.

Hot Tree Editing, your team is my lifeline. You make me work for it, to make each book the best version it can me. Thank you for not taking it easy on me.

Tami, Integrity Formatting, I never worry about what the final product is going to look like with you at the helm. Thank you for making each book beautiful on the inside.

Give Me Books, you never fail me. You take the stress and worry out of release day. I cannot thank you enough for all that you do.

Me beta team, **Stacy**, **Jamie**, **Lauren**. You ladies are not just my beta's, but my friends. I truly value the friendships we've created throughout this journey. I would be lost without you. I will never be able to thank you enough for the time you put into reading my words over and over.

Bloggers, there are so many of you who take the time away from your lives, time away from your families to support authors. Thank you, doesn't seem like enough. You don't get paid to do what you do. It's from the kindness of your heart and your love of reading the fuels you. Without you, without your pages, your voice, your reviews, spreading the word it would be so much harder if not impossible to get my words in reader's hands. I can't tell you how much your never-ending support means to me. Thank you for being you, thank you for all that you do.

My readers, I love you. Not only do you buy my books and read them, you message me along the way. I love hearing from each and every one of you. I love hearing your thoughts as you read, and how the story as a whole touched your life. I'm grateful for ALL of you more than you will ever know. Thank you for taking the time to read my words.

My family, your continued support is beyond measure. I'm so thankful to be living this life with you. I love you.

My Kick Ass Crew, the name of the group, speaks for itself. You ladies truly do KICK ASS! I'm honored to have you on this journey with me. Thank you for reading, sharing, commenting, suggesting, the teasers, the messages all of it. Thank you from the bottom of my heart for all that you do. Your support is everything!

With Love,

Kaylee Ryan
AUTHOR